MARKED BY
DESTRUCTION

The Marked Series

CECE ROSE
G. BAILEY

 Created with Vellum

For everyone who stuck with us, and followed Kenzie's story to the end.

Prologue
MACKENZIE

"*P*lease don't kill me," I whisper. "I haven't done anything to you." In response to my plea, the man brings the silver dagger closer to my throat, his almost grey eyes staring into mine, seeming to assess my every movement.

"Why shouldn't I kill you, Mackenzie Crowe? You opened a portal to my world, risking not only Earth, but Ariziadia too. We had peace, but you broke that peace by trespassing here." he asks me, but I feel like he doesn't want an answer. The marked here have found us guilty without asking, but I will give him a reason anyway.

"If you kill me, no one on Earth or Ariziadia

will be able to stop my father," I say honestly, and he narrows his eyes at me.

"Are you threatening me with your family? If they come here to avenge you, I will simply kill them all," he bites out, a light growl slipping through his words. I try to stay calm and not think about what this marked can shift into.

"I'm not threatening you, only telling you what will happen. He won't come here to avenge me; he wouldn't care if you killed me. If anything, you would be helping him," I say, and I see the confusion cloud over his eyes.

"My father was the one that forced me to open the portal. He was the one behind all of this. He will not stop until he controls Earth. What do you think he will do after he has all of Earth in his control and a marked army with boosted powers from the open portal?" I ask, swallowing a little as the pressure of the dagger against my throat makes it harder and harder to speak. The leader doesn't say anything, just waiting for me to continue.

"He will come here and destroy you. I can stop that, with help from my guys. Now it's your choice," I say, keeping my eyes locked on his and not backing down. I won't plead for his mercy anymore. Marks or no marks, I am stronger than that. He goes to say something when the door slams open behind me. The leader pulls me to his chest, turning me so I can face the open doorway just as Mr Daniels, the twins, East and Enzo walk in.

"Kill or even harm her, and we will burn your world to the ground," Mr Daniels say calmly, but any person would be a fool not to hear the promise of destruction laced in his words.

Chapter 1

MACKENZIE

$\mathcal{W}$aking up shouldn't hurt this damn much, I think to myself as I open my eyes and look above me. The blue sky has sheens of purple and green crossing over it, and there isn't a cloud in sight. The red sun hangs low in sky, leaving me feeling warm despite not having any blankets or even a jacket.

I sit up, looking around at the dark thick grass patch I seem to have landed in. The green field is relatively small, and surrounded by strange, thick trees. They're taller than any trees I've seen before and have leaves hanging down that are bigger than me.

Spotting Enzo across the field of green, right on the edge of the tree line, I try and pull myself up.

As I stand, my ankle immediately gives out, sending me right back onto my ass. I cry out in pain as I clutch it to me, pulling up my dress to assess the damage. After slowly rolling up the dark leggings I still have on under the dress, my eyes burn with tears as I look at the bruised mess my body is in. Not only is my ankle completely bruised a horrible shade of dark purple, but my entire leg seems to be littered with bruises and scrapes. I take a moment to look over the rest of my body, and find that the rest of me doesn't appear to be in great shape either.

"Enzo?" I croak out, but it's so quiet he doesn't even stir. Clearing my throat, I try again. "Enzo!" I shout, swallowing after to clear the dry prickling feeling in my throat. I could really use some water right now. *How long was I even out?*

I hear a groan coming from his direction.

"Enzo!" I shout again, but then I can't stop the coughing fit that follows. I press my hands into the grass, trying to just ride it through. A hand pats my back, and I roll back over, breathing a sigh of relief as I look back into Enzo's dark eyes staring down at me.

"Take it easy, Crowe. You'll cough your lungs up at this rate," he says dryly.

"You're okay," I state, looking over him and see

he looks mostly unscathed despite his slightly torn clothing. He shrugs.

"I wasn't. I healed myself when I first woke up, but I was so wrecked I passed back out before I could make my way to you. I'm sorry, I should have crawled over to fix you first," he says guiltily as he sits down beside me and places his hands on my ankle.

"No, I'm glad you healed yourself first. It's not like I could have," I mutter, looking down at my unmarked skin. I feel his hands warm up as the healing energy from his mark flows through me. A stab of jealousy strikes me at the knowledge that I can't do that anymore. With no healing mark, I have no power to heal anyone. With no marks at all, I'm completely powerless to help anyone, or even defend myself. *How is this possible?*

"Shit, I barely noticed. They haven't re-appeared?" he questions as he runs his dark eyes all over me, as if wanting to check for himself. "I noticed when they disappeared during the fight, but I just assumed they'd come back once you didn't..."

"Once I didn't die?" I supply for him, as he trails off, and then I feel the tears start to trail down my cheeks. *Ryan. How could I even let it slip my mind for a second, much less the minutes I've been awake?*

"Hey, don't cry. It's okay, you're okay. I've got you," he mumbles awkwardly, as he pulls me onto his lap and wipes at my tears with his sleeve.

"He's not okay, Ryan's dead. Alaric killed him...how could he?" I question as the tears continue to flow. I feel the lump in my throat forming, and I feel a headache setting in, but none of that matters.

"Shh, it's okay, just breathe," Enzo says, but his voice is lying. Even he doesn't believe it's okay, nothing is okay. We're trapped on a different world, lost from everyone else but each other, and Ryan is dead. My brother is dead, and my father is the one who killed him.

"It's n-not..." my words are lost in my sorrow, drowned by my cries and the shaking of my body as my entire body racks with sobs against him.

"Get your shit together, Crowe. Breathe. Gods, I'm not good at this..." he trails off. He takes a deep breath before continuing. "Kenzie, listen to me. Crying won't change it, and right now we need to focus if we're going to have a chance at saving everyone else we love. We need to find the others, and then find a way home. And then, we're going to get that son of a bitch and make him pay for what he did. He's going to pay for hurting you, and for taking Ry's life. I promise you that; we won't rest until it's done," he says.

For some reason, whereas softness and reassuring usually makes me want to cry harder, a goal makes the tears stop. It's as if someone cut off whatever supply was fuelling them and left in their place a burning drive to make Alaric pay. I gather my sorrow into a box and shut it, knowing that I can deal with my pain after Alaric is stopped. I swallow thickly and pull myself from Enzo's arms.

"He can't get away with this," I say, and he nods.

"He won't."

"How long do you think we've been here?" I ask, looking around at the unfamiliar landscape. The trees make me think of pictures of rainforests I've seen, but the strangeness of the green and purple in the sky is a firm reminder that this place is not my home world.

"I'm not sure. Too long, I'm dying for some food," he mutters.

"You're hungry?" I ask incredulously. This really isn't a time for snacks.

"A guy's gotta eat," he says with a shrug, but his shinning dark eyes show the real emotion that he hides behind his cool outer facade.

"Let's find water first," I say and then freeze. "Is the water even safe to drink in this world?" I question, and I can feel the crease in my forehead as I really begin to feel the gravity of what being on another world could mean. We both stand, and Enzo walks a little toward the tree line.

"Our ancestors lived here. If they found ways to survive here, so can we. We find water, and then we search for the others. They went through before us, but hopefully they haven't moved far," Enzo says, and I look around. There's no sign of the others being here whatsoever.

"Enzo," I breath, and he looks back at me concerned. "I don't think they landed in the same spot as us. They could be anywhere... Do you have any idea how big Ariziadia is?" I ask. His eyes widen as he too looks around, and sees for himself that there really is no sign of the others.

"I have no idea. Not a fucking clue."

Chapter 2

EAST

"*K*ells, you need to get up," I prod gently, but she continues to ignore me, as she stares off into the distance. She hasn't moved from the edge of the river bank. She was sitting there when I woke up, and she hasn't uttered a word or even acknowledged my or Logan's presence.

I look back at Logan helplessly, and hold my hands up in defeat. He'd suggested I try and talk some sense into her, saying that I'd known her for years longer and was more likely to succeed. He didn't listen when I tried to insist I'd barely spoken to her over those years. I'd mainly stuck to hanging out with Ryan, and she was always with Kenzie.

The pain stabs me in my chest as I think about

Kenzie and Ryan. Ryan because he's gone, and Kenzie... because I don't know if she is. I want to believe she's okay, that Enzo got her out, but I feel the heaviness of loss in my bones when I picture her face. Even if she's okay, I will probably never see her again, not with her being in a whole different world. We don't know if there are people here, or if there is a way to get home. We could be trapped here forever, just the three of us. I look between Logan and Kelly, seeing the blank expression on Kelly's face, and the heart broken one on Logan's as he's clearly thinking along the same lines as I am. Fuck. I stand and walk over to Logan, pulling him away from Kelly so we can talk.

"What the hell are we going to do?" I ask.

"Don't look at me, like, fuck if I know," he snaps back.

"We need a plan. We need to find your brother and Daniels. They fell through when we did, but they were too far away to grab onto..." I say, trailing off as Logan's face pales.

"Do you think they made it through okay? They couldn't have like, gotten lost in between, right?" he questions. I want to tell him that I'm sure they must be here and okay somewhere, but that would be a lie. I have no clue.

"I don't know," I answer honestly, and he nods stiffly as he stretches one arm, and then the other across his chest.

"We need to at least look," he says, casting his eyes around. To one side of us there are mountains, and to the other, thick trees as far as the eye can see.

"Which way should we go?" I ask.

"This way," Kelly's voice calls. She walks towards the mountains, not slowing at all to give us a chance to discuss our options.

"Why that way?" I call after her, but Logan has already begun to follow her.

"I had a vision. We'll find Kenzie this way," she calls back. *Kenzie?* I run after Kelly, grabbing her shoulder and spinning her around to face me.

"What do you mean we'll find Kenzie this way?" I ask. She looks at her shoulder, and I let go, stumbling back as I realise how tightly I must have been holding her. I can see red marks where my fingers were gripping her. "Shit, I'm so sorry," I say quickly, and she waves it off.

"It doesn't matter. Kenzie will need us. We need to get through these mountains. Just trust me, let's go," she says confidently, already turning away and heading in the direction of the mountains once more. Logan moves to step in pace with me.

"Kenzie's okay," he breathes out, the relief in his voice rings clear and matches the way I feel.

"So is your brother, but none of them will be if you two don't hurry up!" Kelly calls back in a chastising tone.

"What about Daniels and Enzo?" I call, already speeding up as we scramble to follow after her.

"Enzo is with Kenzie, but I didn't see Mr D in my vision. I'm sorry."

"Do you think he's okay?" Logan asks as we finally catch up with her again. Gods, this girl can move quickly when she wants to.

"I don't know, but I hope he is. Look, we don't have time for all these questions. We need to keep moving, come on," she says, powering ahead even faster than before. We just about keep up as we trail after Kenzie's curly-haired blonde best friend. Her determined expression gives us both enough hope to trust in her vision, and we follow her without any more questions.

Chapter 3

KENZIE

"There isn't anything but trees, and more trees," I grumble, almost tripping on the vines as we continue to walk through the forest. Enzo grabs my arm, keeping me upright, and then he links his fingers with mine as we keep walking.

"Wait, I have an idea," Enzo stops, seeming as breathless and tired as I am. We have been walking for hours, and both of us are getting exhausted. We really need to find some water soon. I look up, spotting a row of mountains on the other side of the forest as Enzo lets go of my hand. If we can make it through the trees to the other side, then we might be able to find water in the mountains. I lean against a tree as Enzo puts his hands on the ground, digging them into the mud.

"What are you doing?" I ask.

"Using my earth mark to feel for water," he explains and then closes his eyes. We are both silent as he searches, and I stare up at the sky. The massive, red sun is setting, and it's getting dark. I can't see a moon, but I wonder what colour it would be. There are a few stars to be seen, and the sky is a mix of oranges and purples. It's stunning, and I still find it amazing that this world really exists.

"I found something, but it's underground. Come here," he stands up, wiping the mud on his trousers. I step into his arms, giving him a confused look.

"There's a cavern underneath us, with water. I don't sense any other life, so it should be safe, but we need to sink down," he says.

"Through the earth?" I question.

"This isn't earth," he smirks, holding my head to his chest with his one hand, and then using his earth mark to sink us into the ground. When the mud gets up to my neck, I take a deep breath and close my eyes, feeling it slide all over me. I start to panic after a few moments, but then it stops, and we are falling.

"Enzo," I scream, waving my hands around, and then I fall into water. I try to call my marks, on instinct rather than thinking about it, but of course, nothing happens. I swim up, breaking the surface and looking around.

"Enzo!" I shout, hearing splashing to my right. Three balls of fire float up to the top of the cavern, lighting it up. I turn around and see Enzo swimming over to me. When he gets close, he pulls me to him tightly.

"Sorry Crowe, I'm weaker than I thought, and I couldn't call my air mark quick enough," he explains.

"It's okay," I mumble against his chest, looking around at the cave we are in. It's massive, with purple stone walls, and the pool of water is in the middle.

"We can drink this," he tells me, and I don't question him as I immediately lower my head and start drinking.

"Let's get out and dry our clothes. I think we should sleep here for the night," Enzo says.

"What about the others? They will need us," I say, swimming to the edge next to him. He doesn't answer until we both pull ourselves out the pool of water, our clothes dripping onto the purple grass floor.

"Crowe, we didn't see any animals in the forest,

and we were lucky for it. At night, we might not be so lucky. It's too dangerous, the others will know this, and they will find their own place to hide for the night," he says, and I know he's right.

"I just… I'm just worried. They could be anywhere, and my father could be doing anything on Earth," I start panicking as he steps closer to me and pulls me to his chest.

"We could worry all night, or we could rest, get stronger, and find them. I'm all for resting, just so you know," he grumbles, making me chuckle a little as I pull back.

"Okay, so clothes off, and we can hang them over there," I point at the sharp rocks sticking out the wall. I'm sure they will dry. Enzo swallows loudly as I step back, pulling my horrible white dress off, and throwing it to the ground. I'm not drying that. I'm so freaking glad I kept my leggings and vest top on underneath that thing.

I pull my boots off, leaving them on the side as Enzo pulls his shirt off, and I stare at him. His chest is toned, covered in his marks, and there's even a mark just at the bottom of his stomach, disappearing into his jeans. He has a sexy six-pack, and that lickable 'V' dipping below his waist. I look up, and notice that he's breathing more heavily than before.

"I should turn around," Enzo says, but he doesn't. It's a seductive warning, and I feel his dark eyes burning my skin as I lift my top over my head. Leaning down, I push my leggings off slowly as I maintain eye contact with him. When I'm left standing just in my underwear, Enzo finally snaps, walking over to me and picking me up. He slams me into the wall, and I wrap my legs around him.

"Once we do this, Crowe, you're mine. There's no going back," he warns me, his lips tracing lightly over mine as he whispers.

"I was always yours, Enzo," I whisper back, and he slams his lips onto mine crushingly, as his body moulds against me. I can feel the sharp rocks from the cavern wall digging into my back, but he's kissing me so senseless, I couldn't care if I tried. I draw my nails down his back, eliciting a groan from his lips as I press myself firmer against him.

His hands tighten on me, an almost punishing grip, as his lips kiss down my throat. He shifts me higher against the wall before kissing down to my chest. He drags my bra straps down with his teeth, before reaching up a hand behind my back to unclip it. It hits the ground, the sound echoing in the near silence of the place; the only other sound is our thumping heartbeats. He looks down at me, one of his hands tracing down from behind my head and over my neck, his nails scratching softy as he caresses down my throat to my chest. His hands practically glide over my breasts, sinfully teasing as his fingers brush them, leaving me aching for more.

I almost curse as he pulls his hand away from my flaming skin. He steps back, and I unwrap my legs from his waist and slide down, my feet hitting the ground softly as he lowers me. He presses his lips back to mine, kissing me so hard it leaves me utterly breathless, and then he pulls me down with him to the floor.

"What was wrong with against the wall?" I ask between heavy breaths, impressed at the fact I manage to get the words out fairly steady.

"If I fucked you up against the wall, Crowe, it would have been over all too soon. I'm planning to take my time with you. All night, over and over again, until you can't take anymore. I've waited long enough." His hand rests on my shoulder as he pushes me back so I'm lying down completely. He crawls over top of me and looks me straight in the eyes. "Is that a problem?" he adds, his hot breath so close to my lips.

Instead of answering, I lean up a little and kiss him, sliding my hands into his hair and hooking a leg around him, pulling him closer against my body. He kisses me back passionately, his lips demanding to dominate the kiss as he changes the pace. His lips trail off from mine, and he kisses down my throat, before replacing his lips with his hand. He holds my throat gently as he nips my collarbone with his teeth. I moan, my hips bucking a little against him. His grip tightens, and his other hand rests on my hip, his thumb massaging over my hipbone. I feel so fucking connected with him right now. The way he just seems to know exactly where to touch me, it leaves me feeling like a scorching fire that is ready to explode at any minute beneath him.

He peppers kisses down my chest, before circling my left nipple with his tongue, and then the right, biting down on me teasingly. I can't stop the gasp that escapes my lips as he tugs it with his teeth, before kissing it softly and moving back to my left breast. He repeats his tantalising treatment, and then continues his manipulation of my body, working his way down.

As he reaches my waist, he slides across to the hipbone, moving his thumb away to place a kiss there, followed by a nip of his teeth. His thumbs hook into the sides of my underwear, and then he slowly begins to tug them down. He takes his sweet time as he pulls them past my thighs, pausing to brush his fingers up the inside of my left thigh. I shiver, looking down and seeing that his eyes are watching me, watching my reactions to his touch. I bite my bottom lip nervously, hoping he likes what he sees. I suddenly feel so self-conscious with my skin so bare, not even my marks covering me. *I truly feel naked without them.*

"Relax, Crowe, I can feel you shaking," he whispers, his breath hot against the inside of my thigh.

"I'm relaxed, I'm just…I feel a little bare," I reply, feeling the heat from the colour that I know is creeping into my cheeks. He presses a soft kiss to my thigh before moving up my body so that his face is hovering just over mine.

"Generally, people are bare when they're having sex," he says, his lips quirking at the edges.

"It's not that, it's just…" I trail off, moving my hand to brush my fingers over some of his marks. My fingers graze over the one that dips into his jeans, and he draws in a sharp breath.

"You might get them back, Crowe, you never

know. But you're beautiful whether your skin is marked or unmarked, and I'll want you either way. You are fucking perfection," he replies sincerely, settling some of the nerves that were pulsing through me. I wrap a hand behind his neck and pull him close. Kissing him with everything I have, I drop my other hand to his waist to unbutton his jeans.

I slide my hand down his back, and then I use my feet to help remove his jeans and boxers off in one go. Unable to wait anymore, my hand snakes around his hard cock. He groans into my ear as my hand strokes him gently.

"Fuck, Crowe," he whispers, and then I'm flipped over roughly onto my front. One hand grips my left hip firmly, and his nails start to dig in, as I feel his other fingers slide across my entrance, teasingly at first, but then he slides them in and out. He repeats the motion a few times before pulling away. I'm about to protest their absence when I feel him press up against me, and I moan. My hands claw at the rough ground, as I feel him slowly slip inside of me.

My breath is heavy, and as he begins to move, he forgoes his earlier words, losing all control, roughly fucking me from behind. I bite my lip, trying to keep in the moans that are slipping from my lips. He leans down his body closely over my back, his skin warming mine as he kisses the bottom of my neck, tightening his demanding grip on my hip as he does.

Chapter 4

MR M. DANIELS

"*C*ould you walk any fucking slower?" I growl behind me to Locke. He'd been stopping to gape at every little thing as we made our way through the thick forest, and he seems to be determined to continue to gawk as we follow the river up towards the mountains.

"What's the point in rushing? How can you be sure you're even going the right way?" Locke replies, not speeding up in the slightest. Stopping mid-step, I turn around to scowl at him.

"What is the only thing that stands out for miles?" I ask plainly, and he looks around.

"Everything, it's a whole different freaking *world*," he answers, gesturing with his hands out. I feel my teeth grinding together.

"Other than the fact it's a different world, which I'm sure your brother, East, and Kelly are well aware of, what stands out?" I ask again. His eyes fix on the large mountain range we're heading towards.

"Oh," he says.

"Oh," I echo mockingly, before turning on my heel and heading towards the mountains again. I hear Locke jog to catch up with me. *Halle-fucking-lujah.*

"What makes you so sure they would think to go to the thing that stands out, too?" he asks as he reaches my side. I slowly increase my pace, hoping he'll follow suit.

"I'm not holding out hope for your wonder-twin, but I'm hoping that Kelly or East have some sense instilled into them. It's a point that could easily be seen for miles in all directions, and it's the only area that particularly stands out. If they're in a finding distance, they'll head there too," I answer confidently, but the concern they wouldn't think of doing this plays on my mind.

If only Enzo had fallen through, I know he'd think of it.

"Makes sense I guess," Locke replies, but his voice is glum.

"We'll find them," I say, trying to reassure him.

"It's not that, it's just…Ryan's dead, and who

knows what happened to Enzo…or to Kenzie. I haven't been about to stop thinking about her since we got here," he explains, thankfully while keeping up the pace this time.

"Enzo was with her. We have to trust that they will keep each other safe." *He better fucking keep her safe anyway.*

"What if we never see them again?" he asks, and I want to shout at him to shut the hell up. I just want to punch that stupid rock over there, or maybe Locke's face. *Why does he have to keep voicing all my worries?* I try to keep my face calm, and remember that even though there's only a few years age difference between us, Locke has had a much more sheltered life up until recently. I have to be the responsible one here.

"We are going to see them again. The people here were able to cross before, so I'm sure we can find a way home. Or Kenzie will find a way to us. We will find the others, and we will get home to fix this mess," I finally answer, trying to push as much conviction as I possibly can into my words. I look at him, watching the words sink in, and he nods. When he begins to walk again, there's more bounce in his step, and I let out a breath I didn't realise I was holding.

This isn't going to be easy, but I'm damn well going to make it happen anyway.

"What do you know of Ariziadia? I only know a few things I was told as a child," Locke asks me after we walk in silence for a while.

"Not a lot. The council keep everything secret. No one talks about anything they know, and everything is locked up," I say, and he sighs.

"Everyone is going to be mad at the council for hiding this from them. There is no way they could hide the truth now," he says, and he has a point.

"All I know, is that there is a huge book, with far more than twelve pages. An old council member, one of the good ones, told me he suspected that the original marked had more marks than we do. That our blood is so diluted, we have lost the power we originally had," I explain. He suspected a lot of things, like how they could shift into giant creatures, creatures that even dinosaurs feared. He suspected they had their own language, their own religion, and extremely strict rules. He also believed the marked that came to earth, were banished there for doing something bad. That we are all descendants of banished marked, and the marked here wouldn't be happy for any of their children to open a portal. If any of it's true, we have a huge fucking problem, and all I want to do is get back to Earth. Back to Kenzie.

"Then we need to be careful, if we find any marked that are alive here…they could be more powerful than us," Locke muses.

"I won't go down without a fight," I warn him, and he grins.

"Don't worry, I'll be your Robin," he says, and I give him a confused look. *What the fuck is he going on about?*

"Dude, Batman and Robin…come on," he says and shakes his head at me, a disgusted look on his face. "When we get back to Earth and shit is back to normal, I'm forcing you to watch some decent movies."

"Thanks, but no thanks," I mutter.

"You know what Daniels?" he says, patting my shoulder, and I look at his hand, wondering how much Kenzie likes this guy and how pissed she would be if I threw him into the nearby river. "I think we are going to get along just fine," he grins. I don't reply, quickening my pace, but I hear him chuckle behind me as he follows.

Chapter 5

MACKENZIE

"*W*hy are we going this way?" I ask. My feet are killing me, and there's an ache pulsing through the backs of my calves. I seem weaker physically since losing my marks. I never realised how much stronger I'd become when I received them, until they were gone. *Why did Enzo insist on heading up the hill?* I eye the mountains we're slowly approaching, and barely manage to without my groan. *It's only going to get worse!*

"Because this is the most logical way to go, Crowe," he answers simply, but he does slow his pace a little, and he slides his hand into mine. "If Daniels is with the others, or even on his own, he will know to go towards something we can all see for miles."

"Makes sense," I say. We don't talk much more as we climb up the hill, pausing when we get to the top. The top of the hill stretches out into a long field, and the entrance to the mountains is at the other side, not too far away, but that's not what makes me pause.

"What the hell is *that*?" I point at the bottom of the mountains where there's a huge, stone doorway. It's shaped in an arch, with two massive stone tigers that appear to be pushing the doorway as they roar up at the skies. There are people walking in and out, and even horses dotted around, pulling carriage-type things behind them. There's a massive roar, not like anything I've ever heard, and it's loud enough to shake the ground beneath our feet. Enzo grabs me, pushing me behind him before I can see where it came from. I stumble a little, but he holds me to his back.

"Crowe, stay calm, and stay the fuck behind me," he instructs in a nervous voice. I've never heard Enzo nervous, and it scares the shit out of me. I peer my head around his shoulder trying to catch a glimpse of whatever the hell is making that noise. My mouth drops open at the sight of five dragons flying towards us. Four of them are a brown colour, each impressive with their giant

31

wings and long bodies, and there's a grey, almost white, dragon leading the way. He or she is twice the size of the others, with wings covered in deadly looking spikes. *Holy shit…dragons.*

"We should run," I whisper, fear filling me. I don't have any powers, and there is no way Enzo could fight these dragons on his own. They could crush us in a second. What the hell are we going to do?

"It's too late; they've seen us, and there's nowhere to hide around here," he says, and I look behind us, just seeing the fields and hill we have walked up. It's too open, and the treeline is too far away for us to get there in time. Also, we'd be screwed if the dragons shoot fire and we're in those trees.

"Any chance you shift into something big enough to fight these guys?" I ask, watching as the dragon's swoop down, in a formation almost, and land on the field directly in front of us.

"I'm not telling you what I shift into. You'll only laugh, and it sure isn't any use to us here," he says, making me wonder what the hell it is that he shifts into, but I know it's not the time to demand answers. I step around him, and he grabs my hand, stopping me going any further.

"If they are going to kill us, I'm going to be at your side, not hiding behind you," I tell him. "And I love your stubborn, arrogant ass, just in case this is the last time I get to tell you," I add, looking into his dark eyes.

"I'm not saying it now, because it won't be the end of us here," he says, every word is confident.

"See, so stubborn," I mutter, and he grins, lifting my hand and kissing the back of it.

"I believe even when we die, those we love are never separated from us. This isn't the end for us, Crowe," he says, and I don't even get to reply to his sweet words as the dragon in the front roars loudly. The dragons shift back suddenly, until five men are stood about half a mile away from us. They are covered in marks; every visible part of their skin is showing dozens of them. They only have black, woven trousers on, with a gold, v-shaped necklace dipping into the middle of their naked chests. They each also have marks in the middle of their foreheads, which are in the same v shape as their necklaces. They're all tanned, with jet-black hair. I try to stay steady on my feet as the one in the middle steps forward. He holds his hand out and makes a come here gesture.

"We should just go and talk to them, as we can't

run, and they could have killed us by now if that's what they wanted."

"Okay, but for the love of the gods, let me do the talking, Crowe," I give him a shrug for an agreement. "We don't want to piss them off," he mutters, as we start walking towards them. Every step across the field is full of tension and fear. They could easily kill us, and I'm not sure why they haven't already done so. I keep my eyes locked on the one standing in front of the others, clearly, he is the leader. His grey eyes are narrowed on mine, and he doesn't look impressed. We stop when we are close enough to speak, but the dragon man doesn't say a word.

"Do you speak English?" Enzo asks, his voice firm and confident.

"Take them," the leader says, and the guards step forward. Well, I guess they do speak English then.

"Wait!" I step in front of Enzo, who just swears under his breath. The leader holds his hand up, looking at me curiously.

"My name is Mackenzie Crowe. We don't mean you any harm, and we didn't plan to come here. All we want is to find the portal, our friends, and leave," I explain, and for a second he seems curious, but it's gone within a second.

"You opened this portal, and you will pay for the damage you have done. Your *friends'* lives seem a fair price, Mackenzie Crowe," he says and nods at his guard, before turning around and walking away. I start to shout after him when the guards surround us, and my eyes dart back to Enzo.

"Don't fight them, we can't," he says.

The guard to the right of Enzo chuckles and snidely remarks, "Weaklings, all of you."

Enzo smiles and quickly lifts his hand, slamming his fist into the guard's face and he falls to the ground with a thud, knocked out. As the other guards hold Enzo back, he winks at me.

"I thought you warned me not to piss them off?" I ask, as two of the guards grab my arms, and the one on the right pulls a dagger out his pocket, pressing it into my side.

"I told *you* not to piss them off. We both know there was no chance of *me* not doing it," he replies, smirking even as I watch the guards tighten their grip on him.

"No fighting us, or I will kill her," the one holding the dagger warns, and Enzo gives him one sharp nod before walking towards the mountains with the guards holding his arms. *I hope the others don't come here.*

Chapter 6

LOGAN

---

*a*s East and I follow after a confident-looking Kelly, we exchange concerned glances. We don't need to speak to know what the other is thinking right now. Kelly was distraught and practically comatose, the guy she was in love with just died. However, now she's powering up towards the mountains as if we're all having a pleasant hike, and she's eager to get to the end of the trail.

"Kelly, we should probably stop for a minute, and find some water," East calls after her, breaking the tense silence between us all. She carries on like she hasn't heard him, but if anything, she's sped up a little.

"Kelly!" I yell, trying to get her attention, but

she keeps right on walking. "Kelly, stop!" I shout louder, grimacing at the irritation I hear in my own voice.

"We don't have time to stop," she shouts back, not even turning around to face us. I groan as I take in the steep climb ahead of us. East and I only got a couple of hours sleep last night. She'd woken us up before first light, and practically dragged us back onto the path. I'm pretty sure she didn't even sleep for those few hours, because whenever I'd stirred I had seen her pacing. *How is she functioning without sleep for so long?* I notice East isn't walking beside me anymore and turn back to him, seeing him frozen in place staring up at the sky.

"East?" I call, stepping back towards him, but he doesn't answer, just keeps staring up. "Are you okay?"

"Is it me, or is there a fucking dragon in the sky?" he asks incredulously, pointing up above us. My head shoots up, my eyes searching the skies for something impossible, and damn if they don't find it. In the distance is what most definitely looks like a dragon. *Fucking hell, I hope it doesn't breathe fire.*

"It's definitely a dragon, and unless you two want to meet it, hurry up!" Kelly shouts back at us, still pressing ahead.

"Aren't you walking in the direction of the dragon?"

"We're going through a gap in the mountains. It won't see us if you two would just *hurry up* like I keep asking you to do," she snaps, spinning around on the spot to glare at us, her hands on her hips and eyes blazing.

"Wouldn't we be better covered by the trees back there?" East questions. "Away from the flying dragon?" he adds, his eyes darting up nervously to the gigantic beast that's flying around high in the sky near to the mountains.

"We have to go this way, and we have to go *now*. Or else we'll miss them, and then Kenzie and Enzo won't make it without you guys," she explains haughtily, before turning and carrying on.

"Wait, miss who? Locke? You know where my brother is?" I call, racing after her to make her explain.

"Yes, I know where Locke is, and you better hurry up before someone kills him," she answers as I reach her, rolling her eyes. I can hear East running up after us from behind, clearly having decided to follow Kelly towards the threat in the sky after all.

"Someone's trying to kill him?" I ask, my eyes

widening in alarm. She laughs, but it's a hollow sounding laugh. Empty.

"Relax, it was a joke. He's driving Mr Daniels completely insane, and he may or may not be muttering under his breath about ways to silence your brother," she answers.

"You can see all that?" East asks curiously, catching up to us and walking on her other side.

"I can see everything," she whispers. "It's so strange. My vision here seems amplified. I can see all of us, every possibility, every path we could take, and ones I couldn't even imagine before. I can see where we are now, where we've been, and all the places we could go from here. I can see him too…" her voice waivers off, and she coughs awkwardly. "Ignore me. Anyway, yes, I can see them. We're getting close." She speeds up again, powering ahead as if she's trying to lose us.

I share another concerned look with East. Both of us can easily guess who the "him" is that she's referring to.

There's only one mark that gives the gift of communing with some of the dead, and Kelly doesn't have the spirit mark. I can't imagine Ryan's spirit would be one to stick around either.

"We need to watch her," East says quietly, and I nod silently in agreement.

"I saw that too," Kelly shouts back in an irritated voice, and East's eyes bulge. "I'll forgive you, if you two would just hurry up!" she adds with a yell. We both speed up, trusting that even if she is confused from grief right now, that she's clear enough to be telling us the truth about Kenzie and the others. We have to get wherever it is we need to be for them, and quickly.

AFTER NARROWLY AVOIDING STUMBLING over a rock, I continue walking behind Kelly through a dark, damp pathway through the mountain. A pathway that looks long forgotten by the rest of Ariziadia. East steps closely behind me, and I can't stop the snigger that escapes me when I hear him stumble over the rock.

"Could have warned me," he mutters.

"Warned you about what?" I ask not so innocently.

"Wanker." He shoves my back lightly.

"Shhh!" Kelly urges us to be quiet.

"What?" I whisper in response.

"Just wait," she answers, a little glee slipping into her voice. We turn a corner, and Kelly darts forward, turning and pressing her back against the wall, just as a figure smacks me to the ground. Another knocks East to the ground at the same time. Kelly laughs from where she's standing against the wall.

I pull my arm back, ready to fight back, when I see my attacker's face above mine. A face that's just like mine. "Locke?"

"Logan? How did you find us?" he asks, giving me a one-armed hug as he pulls me up from the ground. I look over and see Daniels helping East up.

"Glad you three are alive," Daniels says, nodding at us.

"As sweet as this reunion is, we don't have time for it," Kelly says impatiently, any humour she'd had a second ago already gone.

"And you're back to that." I turn to her, giving her a glare. "Why don't you just tell us what we are rushing around for?"

"You need to save Kenzie and Enzo," she answers plainly.

"Well how are we going to do that when we can't get back to Earth?" Locke asks, sounding confused. I swallow thickly, not wanting to be the one to explain that Enzo and Kenzie are stuck here too. Luckily, Kelly has no such qualms.

"Kenzie and Enzo fell through, too. They've been separated, and some guy has a knife to Kenzie's throat, or he will in about thirty minutes.

"What?!"

"Knife?!"

"You can't be…"

"Fucking serious?" everyone seems to exclaim at once, as we all turn to Kelly.

"So, here's the plan," she begins, ignoring all our concern as she continues to explain calmly. "I'm going to distract the people, and then you guys are going to sneak down to the building in the centre with the red roof. You'll grab Enzo from the entrance hallway where he's being held by two guards, and then continue into the main chamber save Kenzie. Are we all clear?" she asks.

"What people?" Locke asks.

"And where is this building?" East adds.

"I don't have time to explain. Do you all trust me?" she asks, and begrudgingly we all nod. Of course we trust her on this, she cares about Kenzie just as much as we do. "Great, now follow me."

Chapter 7

LOGAN

"Five, four, three, two, one..." Kelly starts randomly counting down as she peeks through the small gap between the wall and the door. I look around the small storage space as Kelly swears under her breath and starts counting again. She has been doing this for the last half an hour, and none of us know what to say to her. We agreed to trust her, but I think she is losing her god damn mind.

"What do you keep doing that for? Why are you counting?" I finally snap, and she turns sharply to me.

"For the distraction to come. They have been stopped outside, but my timing is off," she mutters, and her eyes almost seem to glow a white colour for a second before she shakes her head.

"What is the distraction? You haven't told us anything!" I whisper harshly, and Locke places his hand on my chest, stopping me from going over to Kelly and shaking the shit out of her.

"Remember, I distract, and you all go to get Enzo, so don't follow me out. I will catch up," she says and starts counting again. This time when she gets to one, she opens the door, and walks out like she hasn't got a care in world. I dart forward, peeking out the door when it shuts behind her, and my mouth drops open at what distraction Kelly has planned.

"She is crazy, fucking crazy," I mutter, making all the guys run over to the door to catch a glimpse of what I'm seeing. Kelly is sneaking around behind what can only be described as a holding pen on wheels. Inside the pen are five creatures, that look similar to horses, but they are not. They have two large spikes on their heads, black fur covering their huge bodies, and feet that look big enough to squash your head. They have long noses like horses, with large eyes that glow red.

"Is she letting them out?" East questions, and I

shrug my shoulders. *I don't have a clue.* Kelly leans down, picking the lock with a knife she just happens to have, and it snaps open just as some people walk past. I watch, holding my breath as she hides behind the pen, and thankfully, the people keep walking without seeing her or the broken lock. When they are gone, she goes back to the front of the cart, pulling off the chains and opening the doors. I watch as she reaches into her pocket, pulling out a lighter, and flicking it on. *Where the hell did she get that from?*

The creatures all turn towards her rapidly, like they can sense the flame. The one nearest Kelly steps forward, pressing its nose into the fire, and the fire spreads all over its body like he is covered in petrol. The fire spreads from creature to creature, but it's not hurting them. It's like they are making themselves set on fire and they all seem happier in the flames. The creatures never take their eyes off Kelly and the flame. It's almost like the flame is controlling them. An alarm rings, sounding like a horn, just as Kelly waves the lighter in the air and runs off down one of the corridors, with the creatures running after her.

"That girl knows how to cause one hell of a distraction, that's for sure," Logan mutters as we watch dozens of Ariziadian people run off in the direction Kelly just left in.

"She's Kenzie's best friend; did you honestly expect her not to be a little bit crazy?" East says. Daniels nudges me out of the way, waiting until the last person jogs past us before stepping out the room.

"This way, we won't have much time. If we see anyone, we will have to knock them out, but make sure not to kill anyone. We need these people to get home and killing their people won't make their leader listen to us," Daniels warns us, and then sprints off down the corridor before any of us can agree to his plan. I run after him, with East and Locke at my sides. The corridors are empty; the sound of crashing and shouting can be heard behind us, but that only means Kelly's distraction is working. I stop when I run into Daniels' outstretched arm, and he puts a finger to his mouth to shush me. I look around him, seeing Enzo standing in the middle of two guards who are waiting just outside a pair of double doors.

"I'll take the one on the right," Mr Daniels says, and he jumps out from behind the wall. I call my air power, slamming it into the guard on the left and pushing him away from Enzo. He gets up quickly, as

East comes to my side. East slams a wave of water into the guard, who pushes it out of the way likes it's nothing.

"They are stronger than us with their marks, just punch them!" Enzo shouts, and I turn for a second to see him, Daniels and Locke struggling to push past the wall of air the marked are using. East grins, running and jumping straight at the guard in front of us. I use my air mark to knock his feet from under him, and East lands straight on his chest, his fist smacking in the guard's face before he can call his marks to stop East's hit from landing.

"Marks or not, that has to hurt," I say glancing at the passed-out guard.

"Crowe is in there, hurry! They're going to kill her!" Enzo shouts at us, running towards the door, with us all following and praying they haven't touched Kenzie. If they've hurt her, whether they have more marks than us or not, we will find a way to burn this world to the ground.

Chapter 8

MACKENZIE

*A*s we are led into the mountain, I try not to show just how interesting I find the place. We know so little about the marked that live in Ariziadia, and yet, they seem to know something of us. The way they're watching me and Enzo so intently as they lead us through says it all. Like it's the Red Sea, people part out of our way as we walk along a path that leads us deep into the heart of the mountain. I look above us for the source of light, noticing just how bright it is in the mountain, even this far in, and I can't see any torches or electricity. The entire mountain seems just as light as it is outside. *How is this possible?*

I turn my attention to the marked walking with us. They look less scary in human form than they did dragon, but still, I remain cautious. Without my powers, I'm practically useless. The some of the marks covering their skin are unlike any I've seen before, but they have some similar ones, too. From looking at just three of the men, I can see they seem to carry all eleven of the marks we have. I can't spot the twelfth mark on any of them, but they could easily be hidden under their black trousers. One of the marks I don't recognise looks like a mask. *I wonder what that one does?* Do these other marks really symbolise other powers, or are the marked here just fans of tattoos that resemble marks?

"This way," the leader indicates, gesturing for us to take a left turn. We're led back out into natural sunlight, and my jaw drops at what I see now that we've walked through the mountain. The light that glistens off the buildings is almost blinding, and the sheer amount of structures packed and hidden away in the middle of the mountains is unbelievable. It's like they've dug down into the ground in the centre of a circle of mountains and built a mini-city in here. If you didn't know where the entrance was, and if you didn't climb to the top of the mountain to check, you'd never see this place; it's so perfectly hidden. *But what are they hiding from?*

"Holy shit," Enzo mutters.

"This is insane," I say in agreement. We don't get long to gawk though, as we're roughly dragged down some stone steps towards the buildings. "Where are you taking us?" I ask, earning myself an annoyed look from Enzo.

"You don't get to ask questions here, Mackenzie Crowe," the leader answers before any of the others can speak. I go to speak again, but I'm cut off by another irritated look from Enzo. I slam my mouth shut and nod at him, accepting that for now, he's probably right and I really should shut up.

We're guided silently through the mini-city, and it feels like we're being taken right into the heart of the place, towards the very central building. The central building doesn't reflect the light as the other buildings do. Its roof is a deep red, and it's shorter than the rest of the buildings, but spans much longer.

We're led to that building, and I'm pulled ahead of Enzo as we walked single file through a corridor.

"You will wait here," one of the men grunts to Enzo, as the others continue to lead me further into the building.

"Like hell am I letting you take her," he growls, his black eyes burning, and he starts forward, clenching his fists. I look over at all the marked surrounding us, and take a deep breath.

"Just leave it, Enzo. Please?" I plead. There are just too many of them. I try to communicate with my eyes that we can't take them all. Our best bet is to try and reason with them. I can try and talk sense with whoever they're taking me to see. He nods, begrudgingly leaning back against the wall, and two of the guards stop to stand either side of him, while I'm led deep into the heart of the building.

"You will go in here," the leader says, and I nod. Shakily, I reach out and push the large, ornately decorated door open. I walk into the large chamber, flaming torches lighting themselves as I walk down towards a large throne. On the throne, I can barely make out a shadowed figure sitting there.

As I reach about halfway into the room, the figure fades into nothing. I turn around, seeing the door slam closed. I swallow the lump in my throat.

"Mackenzie Crowe, I would say welcome to Ariziadia, however, you are not a guest here, but merely a trespasser," a voice whispers from right behind me. I quickly turn and find myself looking into grey eyes.

"I don't even want to be here. So how about

you just let me find my friends, and then we can all leave," I offer, and the man steps even closer.

"You wish to return to Earth?" he questions.

"Yes, yes I do," I answer.

"Do you even realise why some of our people chose to go to Earth?"

"No, nobody knows anymore," I answer truthfully.

"Are you not curious as to why your people have so few of the marks that we have here?" he questions me again.

"Until today I didn't know that you all had these marks. We didn't know any other than the twelve, and most people don't even know what the twelfth mark does." I answer him honestly.

"Your people are so clueless. Have you truly forgotten everything?" he asks, and I shrug, not sure what more I can tell him. He sighs and continues to explain. "Our people were at war with each other, long ago. To bring an end to the feud peacefully, they agreed they would move to another world. A world where they could live how they wished, and we could live how we wished. We chose segregation to stop bloodshed.

The leader of your people was exceptionally gifted, and she had every power a marked can be bestowed with. She had the power to build bridges between worlds. Using her gifts of divination, she found a suitable world, one with beings much like us. There were key differences though, unmarked skin and no powers. with no powers. They decided to blend in this new world, they would have to give up some of their power, or risk being discovered by the native species. A species known for being hostile towards those that are different."

"The people gave up their powers willingly?" I ask incredulously, completely unable to fathom why someone would give their powers away. I look down at my bare skin on my arms, my marks gone. I would never give my powers up if I had a choice. Mine were ripped from me, just as my brother was.

"They agreed they would keep just eleven of the powers. The leader used her gifts to mute all of your magic and to repress the other gifts. The plan was that eventually, you would give up all of your powers. The eleven you kept were to help you settle. Earth to build and grow crops, technomancy to have the tools to survive. Fire to keep you warm, water to keep you hydrated. Divination to see threats coming for you… you get the idea, yes?" he asks, and I nod in understanding. "We agreed with them that this seemed like a reasonable solution. So, they left our world behind, and we have lived in peace amongst our own kind ever since, leaving you to your own devices."

"I can't believe this," I whisper, and my eyes widen when I see him pull a silver dagger from a sheath against his forearm. "What are you…" I trail off, stepping back away from him, panicking as I'm completely powerless without my marks. He quickly closes the distance, pressing the dagger against my throat.

"Please don't kill me," I whisper. "I haven't done anything to you." In response to my plea, the man brings the silver dagger closer to my throat, his almost grey eyes staring into mine, seeming to assess my every movement.

"Why shouldn't I kill you, Mackenzie Crowe? You opened a portal to my world, risking not only Earth, but Ariziadia too. We had peace, but you broke that peace by trespassing here." he asks me, but I feel like he doesn't want an answer. The marked here have found us guilty without asking, but I will give him a reason anyway.

"If you kill me, no one on Earth or Ariziadia will be able to stop my father," I say honestly, and he narrows his eyes at me.

"Are you threatening me with your family? If

they come here to avenge you, I will simply kill them all," he bites out, a light growl slipping through his words. I try to stay calm and not think about what this marked can shift into.

"I'm not threatening you, only telling you what will happen. He won't come here to avenge me; he wouldn't care if you killed me. If anything, you would be helping him," I say, and I see the confusion cloud over his eyes.

"My father was the one that forced me to open the portal. He was the one behind all of this. He will not stop until he controls Earth. What do you think he will do after he has all of Earth in his control and a marked army with boosted powers from the open portal?" I ask, swallowing a little as the pressure of the dagger against my throat makes it harder and harder to speak. The leader doesn't say anything, just waiting for me to continue.

"He will come here and destroy you. I can stop that, with help from my guys. Now it's your choice," I say, keeping my eyes locked on his and not backing down. I won't plead for his mercy anymore. Marks or no marks, I am stronger than that. He goes to say something when the door slams open behind me. The leader pulls me to his chest, turning me so I can face the open doorway just as Mr Daniels, the twins, East and Enzo walk in.

"Kill or even harm her, and we will burn your world to the ground," Mr Daniels say calmly, but any person would be a fool not to hear the promise of destruction laced in his words.

Chapter 9

MACKENZIE

The marked keeps the dagger pressed against my throat as I look at Mr Daniels, the twins, East, Enzo, and finally Kelly, who walks in the room after them. She doesn't even look at me as she steps into the middle of the room, holding her hands together and blocking my view of the guys. The blade scrapes against my neck as I breathe, and in response, Enzo calls his fire mark, setting his hands alight. *This isn't going to end well.*

"You will let her go. I have already seen it," Kelly says, stopping right in front of us but looking only at the marked man. "We're wasting time when we all have other more *important* things to do," Kelly states calmly. The room becomes still, silent except for the sound of our breathing as we wait for him to decide whether to kill me or let me go. I'm not expecting it when he moves the dagger away and suddenly throws me away from him with his other arm. I fall on the floor near Kelly's feet, and East runs over, helping me up, though Kelly walks around me like I'm not even there.

"What do you see?" the marked asks Kelly, who tilts her head to the side. Her motions are almost robotic, like she has planned every movement before it happens. *In other words, she's acting bat-shit crazy.*

"War. Death. Destruction. It will come for both worlds if you ignore my warning, King Elnam," she says coldly, and King Elnam looks between us all. His cold, grey eyes seem to see something in the way we stare back at him, or at least, in the way Kelly seems so confident.

"Close the door, and we shall talk," he says, walking over to the only seat in the room and sitting down.

"Are you okay?" East asks me, as the twins shut the door, and Enzo comes to my side, stroking my arm with his hand.

"I'm fine. Well, as fine as I can be," I mutter in response. Mr Daniels walks to Kelly's side, his hand brushing mine as he passes me, but I know we don't have time to catch up right now. The twins stay near the door, giving me protective looks when I look their way.

"We do not welcome Earth marked here. It is not our way, and my people will want your heads for opening the portal," King Elnam starts and drifts his eyes towards me, "But we will not ignore the warnings of our seers. We treasure them above all else."

"Have your own people seen the future?" I ask.

"Yes, and we know destruction is a kind word for what the future is showing us all. It seems we were wrong in our belief that the portal being opened was the destruction we have all feared," King Elnam tells us. "But when I held you, Mackenzie Crowe, I saw your father. I saw him sitting on my throne, with my people dead at his feet."

"How did you know he was my father?" I ask.

"He had you at his side, tied up with empty, lifeless eyes. He called you his daughter as he asked you to kill another one of my people," he says, glaring at me like I've already done it. I shiver as I take a step back, the fear of my father controlling me like that terrifying to me. I won't let him live long enough to control anyone ever again.

"Then let me go back. Let me stop him because you know I am the only one that can. He killed my brother, took my marks, and I will kill him for that. I promise you," I swear to him.

"No," Kelly is the one that responds. At her demanding tone I freeze, looking towards her. I move away from East and the others, walking over to Kelly's side, needing to talk to her. I move to touch her arm, but she jumps away from me, bumping into Mr Daniels before standing up straight again.

"Kells?" I mumble, confused, and her tear filled eyes meet mine for only a second before she looks away.

"Mackenzie will need her marks back in order to close the portal, so she must enter the Zarrci Honzel," Kelly says, and then translates whatever the hell she just said to us as she looks back. "The waters of the pure. It's a place where the Ariziadian people believe their powers come from. It can bring back Mackenzie's powers."

"How the fuck do you know that?" Enzo asks.

"She knows everything. Ariziadia is boosting her powers, her connection. It happens with some of our kind. They can bond with the very magic that makes us marked," King Elnam tells us, his eyes watching Kelly closely like she is fascinating.

"We need a moment to talk…alone," Mr Daniels says, stepping around Kelly and wrapping an arm around my waist to make it clear who he wants to speak with.

"I will speak to my people as well. You will need supplies to make it to Zarrci Honzel alive," King Elnam drawls, already standing up, and heading to the door.

"I will come with you," Kelly says, moving to follow him. I grab her arm as she passes me, and I hold on tight because I can't have her look at me like this. I can't have her ignoring me. I want to hold her and tell her it will all be okay, but nothing leaves my mouth for a moment as I stare at her.

"Don't do this, look at me, Kelly. Please," I beg her, and when she does, the pain in her eyes makes me want to look away. She looks so lost; her blue eyes seem empty of anything other than pain.

"You remind me of him, Kenz. You look too much like him, you sound too much like him… please let me go," she pleads, her voice cracking with every word, and I let go of her arm as my own eyes fill with tears. I nod once, and she walks out the room, following the king without looking back once at us.

"Come here. She doesn't mean it, and it won't be like this forever. I am so sorry for your brother's death," Mr Daniels says, pulling me to his chest as I burst into tears. I feel someone else rubbing my back, and then other hands on my shoulders, in my hair, until I know all my guys are close and comforting me.

"We will avenge his death, we promise you that Kenz," East tells me, his grief and anger coming through his words. Ryan was his best friend. He's lost someone important, too, and here he is, trying to just comfort me.

"I can't talk about Ryan right now. I can't focus on him, or I will break down and give up," I whisper, wiping my tears on Mr Daniels' shirt. "Sorry, I got your shirt all wet."

"Not a problem, Kenzie," he says, kissing my forehead. I turn, still somehow staying in his arms as I face my guys. They all look tired and worried, and yet, they look at me like nothing else matters.

"We have no choice but to trust this king and go where he wants. I trust Kelly, she wouldn't send us to our deaths," I say to them.

"I don't know trust I her right now, she isn't fully herself..." Locke says, and Logan hits his arm.

"For Ryan, she wouldn't let Kenzie die. But more than that, she knows Kenzie and us, and she knows we are the only ones who stand a chance of killing Alaric," East replies firmly, and the others mumble their agreements. The door is opened before we can talk or plan anymore. Kelly and the king walk in, but Kelly stays near the door.

"Have you made your decision?"

"You don't have to play games. It's not like we never had a choice. We will go and return my marks," I say, stepping in front of my guys. For the first time since my brother died, I have the tiniest amount of hope that I can get him his revenge.

Chapter 10

MACKENZIE

"You want us to do what now?" I ask the Ariziadian marked incredulously, as I shift the leather backpack I'd been given on my shoulders. They'd given us each a leather backpack with some supplies for our trip. I'd taken a quick peek inside and noticed a small box I'd yet to open, an old-fashioned water canteen–with no water in it–and enough food for only a day, at most. Clearly, they expected us to find our own.

I glance nervously around the courtyard where we're waiting for our escort. The other Ariziadian marked are sitting on the far side of the courtyard, seeming to be avoiding us. Which, considering their king's vision, I suppose couldn't blame them.

"We want you to ride us," he replies, not seeing the issue with his wording. Locke however, thinks it's hilarious, and is in fits of laughter behind us.

"Sorry, mate, you're not really my type," he jokes. Only Logan laughs. I'm not sure if it's more of a twin sympathy laugh, or if they've just got a similar, albeit awful, sense of humour.

The Ariziadian marked looks at Locke curiously. "I do not understand? You have a preference of which of us to ride in dragon form?" he questions.

"Wait, you shift into fucking *dragons*? You're the dragons that Logan and East saw flying around?" he questions in disbelief.

"Did I not mention that the marked that grabbed us turned into dragons?" I ask innocently, batting my eyelashes ridiculously as I turn to face him.

"You left that out on purpose!" he accuses me, and I grin.

"Maybe," I say, dragging the word out as I turn to face the Ariziadian marked.

"So, you're going to fly…and we're all just going to what, ride on your backs? Do you have harnesses? Seats? Something to hold onto so we don't plummet to our painful deaths?" I ask, while picturing just how high a dragon could fly. *Fuck, why do we have to ride the damn dragons?* The marked laughs at my questions, clearly finding it highly amusing how nervous I am to hop onto a dragon's back and soar through the sky. My eyes narrow. "It's not funny," I snap.

"It's very funny. You Earth marked are so strange. And quite rude as well. You haven't even asked for my name, and yet, you expect me to fly you to the edge of the path to Zarrci Honzel," he says, folding his arms. His bulging arms. *Gods, why are the marked here so huge?* East decides to save me from further embarrassment, and he steps up so he is in line with me.

"You haven't asked for our names either," East says to him, and the man smiles.

"I know all of your names. Mackenzie Crowe, Easton Elias Black, Locke & Logan Valentine, Enzo Langston, and—"

"Look, we get the idea. You know our names," Enzo cuts him off in an irritated voice, and I quickly glare at him for being rude before turning back to the marked.

"What's your name?" I ask.

"Taelon," he answers with a smile.

"So, Taelon, why are you so chatty compared to

your friends back there?" Logan asks, gesturing to the other Ariziadian marked that are still hovering right on the other side of the courtyard.

"Not all of us think it is a bad thing that you are here," Taelon answers with a shrug. "Now Earth beings, are you ready to fly?" he asks, and I look around again for any sign of Kelly.

"I don't think she's coming, Kenz," East says gently, wrapping an arm around my shoulders. I sigh, snuggling into his side for warmth.

"I know, it's just hard," I mumble quietly.

"You are sad your seer friend did not come to see you off?" Taelon asks curiously, and I nod. "She is very gifted, far more gifted than we would expect any of your seers to be. She's also gifted with healing, is she not? It's very strange in our world to meet someone with just two marks, but to have so much power within those two marks, that's even stranger. Here someone with only two marks would be seen as defective. I'm not sure if it's even happened before. I once heard of a man with only five," he comments, and I bite my tongue. I don't like how he's talking about Kelly, but we need their help. I need my marks back, so I can fight my father.

"You okay, Crowe?" Enzo asks, and I jerk my head in a stiff nod, not trusting my voice.

Taelon, seemingly done with the conversation after my sudden silence, walks back over to the other Ariziadian marked. One by one, the four men shift into large dragons, forms much bigger than their human ones. I realise quickly the numbers don't quite add up.

"How are we doing this?" I ask, looking between the guys.

"Kenzie can—

"I'll take—

I look between Logan and Daniels, who'd both spoken at once. "Maybe I want my own dragon. Why don't you two share a dragon?" I ask.

"Well, seeing as all of us have an air mark, it makes sense for you to come with one of us. Just in case, Crowe. Can't have you falling without one of us to catch you," Enzo answers for them. I hate to admit he has a point. I sigh.

"I can take, Kenz," East offers.

"I don't mind taking you either," Enzo says to me. Turning to face Locke, I cross my arms over my chest.

"You going to offer, too?" I ask, feeling like the shiniest toy in the box.

"Nah, I want my own dragon. I am going to try and convince him to do loops and stuff," he admits, making us all laugh.

"Are you *really* that attached to Locke? I mean, you have another that looks just like him," Daniels questions in an exasperated voice.

"Hitting me right here, man," Locke says, mimicking himself being stabbed in the chest humorously.

"Yes, I'm very attached," I answer with a tight smile.

"Then you should go with Locke. He's less likely to do something stupid with you to look after," he replies, and Locke doesn't look thrilled. I nudge him in the stomach playfully as I walk past him and towards the hulking dragons.

"Being stuck with me won't be *that* bad," I tease, and he jogs to catch up with me, sliding his arm around my waist as he reaches me. I feel his hot breath against my neck and shiver.

"Being stuck with you was my plan the whole time," he whispers in my ear quietly. I pull back and look at him, seeing the devious grin and playful look in his eyes.

"Sneaky. I like it," I reply, leaning up to kiss him. I'd intended just a quick, light kiss, but Locke isn't having any of that. He pulls me up against him tightly and crushes his lips to mine. I mould right into him, forgetting that we have a scaly audience waiting for us.

A loud, impatient roar reminds me of their presence, and I sigh, turning around to face the dragons. Trying to appear confident as I walk up to them, I stride quickly towards the dragon that I think is Taelon, but I can't stop my eyes from widening a little at the sheer size of him. The fact they really don't have harnesses, or anything else to hold onto, doesn't help my anxiety either.

"Ladies first," Locke says in a humorous tone, seeing my hesitance to climb up onto the beast. I roll my eyes at him, before realising I have no idea how I'm supposed to actually get up onto the dragon.

East notices my predicament and uses his air mark to lift me up into the air and safely deposit me onto the dragon's back. I shoot him a grateful smile as Locke uses his own power to bring himself up, and he rests his arms around my waist. I watch the others as they each get onto a different dragon's back.

I rest my hands tentatively on the dragon and notice that the skin beneath my hands doesn't feel slimy like I'd expected. The scales feel pretty smooth, but a little cool to the touch. I look around for something to grip onto, and spot a sharp ridge at the top of his back, where his neck meets it. Hesitating before grabbing on, I freeze staring down at it, my hands half out-stretched. *Should I hold onto that, or is it frowned upon?*

My decision is made for me when the dragon just lurches up into the air, and my hands slam down onto the ridge, gripping it so tightly my knuckles go white. Its wings have stretched out into a massive wingspan that I couldn't have imagined it having. The dragon's wings curl as it builds up air underneath them, before launching itself even higher into the sky, the air slamming into us the higher it soars. As the dragon finally evens out in the air, I realise how tightly Locke is gripping my waist and smile. He won't be asking for loops and turns anytime soon.

"This is incredible!" Locke shouts in my ears, needing to shout over the air rushing over us.

"Terrifying!" I correct him, trying not to look down. I really don't need to see how high we are right now.

"Terrifyingly incredible," he amends, and I feel the rumble of his chest as he laughs behind me. I close my eyes tight and just feel the air flowing around us. My stomach lurches every time the dragon drops or rises like a damn rollercoaster.

Opening them again, I finally look around and see the world below us, looking so much smaller with how high we are. I take in the strange landscape, and I feel my body relax a little, having to remember to keep holding on, as I finally let myself just enjoy the ride.

Chapter 11

MACKENZIE

*S*tanding unsurely at the edge of the forest we've landed beside, I watch as Taelon shifts back into human form. He smiles warmly at us once he finishes the shift.

"Enjoyed the journey?" he asks.

"Surprisingly, yes," I answer, while glancing around us. "So, which way is it to the Zarrci Honzel?" I add, not exactly seeing a sign.

He gestures to a large stone by the edge of the forest. "That is the starting point, but there are no other directions," he says simply, and the guys practically explode in outrage.

"No way," Enzo says stiffly.

"How do we know that this forest leads anywhere?" East questions.

"We're meant to just trust you?" Logan asks.

"We can't take a risk like that. There's no proof that there is anything but danger if we follow your direction, not that you've really given us any," Daniels states.

"This is the way of our marked kind. All of our people must find the way themselves from this point forward," Taelon explains, and I can see the tension in him as he does. He doesn't like being questioned like this.

"Look guys, we don't really have another choice," I begin, but I'm cut off by a dark look from Daniels.

"There is always another choice, Kenzie," he says firmly.

"You may not trust this guy, but I have faith in Kelly," I reply, standing my ground. We are going to look for this damned Zarrci Honzel. I need my powers back so that I can fight. I refuse to be help-less like this forever.

"Are you sure?" Logan asks me, and I nod.

"I know Kelly is going through things," I say, taking a moment to try and stop myself from thinking about the reason she is feeling so low and out of sorts. If I let myself think about him, I'll be useless to everyone. "She wouldn't tell us this was the way if it wasn't. We need to trust her."

"This is for you. It will help you listen," Taelon says, thankfully moving the conversation away from the awkward point it had reached. He pulls out a small silver looking tube. It's about the size of my arm, and it seems heavy.

"Listen? Listen to what?" I ask.

"To the marks," he answers cryptically, and places the tube in my hand. I nearly drop it because it's so much lighter than it looks. I turn the silver tube over in my hands a few times, looking at the unfamiliar symbol etched on it. The symbol is a circle, with ten straight lines escaping out the centre.

"Good luck, Mackenzie. Do not worry, if you and your men die, we will bury your bodies in a respectful way," he says calmly, like it's a normal and reassuring thing to say and not really, really weird.

"Err...thanks," I reply awkwardly, watching as he turns around and runs, shifting back into his dragon form and shooting into the skies with his friends following suit.

"We forgot to ask how we are supposed to get back to them, and to Kelly, when this is all over,"

Mr Daniels growls in frustration. I slide the tube into my jacket pocket and peer up at the stone.

"We didn't have any *chance* to ask, and I have a feeling they wouldn't tell us anyway. We need to get to this place, and get my marks back. Let's focus on one thing at a time," I say, placing my hand on his arm. He takes my hand, kissing the back of it gently, and linking our fingers.

"You're right, one thing at a time. Everyone should still be on guard though, we don't know this world," Mr Daniels warns, and the guys all nod their agreement. Enzo and East walk in front as we head into the forest, and the twins stay behind us. I keep my eyes on the trees as we pass them. It's amazing how different they are to anything I've seen. It's like the roots make up the main part of the tree, and the leaves sprout out the roots all the way up them. There are dozens of bright pink and blue flowers dotted around, and even the grass has strange little blue bugs moving through them.

"What do you think Alaric is up to?" I ask, and I'm met with only silence in response. Mr Daniels looks down at me for a second, rubbing his thumb over my wrist in a soothing notion as he replies.

"The plan was to take the academy first. Once he has full control of the academy, he will attack the

London council, then every other council after that. If all the councils fall, he will be the only leader and he'll have full control over all of the marked," he explains, and it makes sense. The quickest way to bring us down would be to get rid of the most powerful of us. The councils. Our leaders. Without them, it would be chaos.

"And then what?" East asks, clearly listening in, and a quick glance around suggests all the guys are listening as they watch us.

"Then he will attack the human governments, the human royals, the human leaders with his marked army. He plans to take over the entire Earth," Daniels says, and I rest my head on his shoulder as we get follow along the edge of the forest and the large stone comes into view again.

"He will destroy everything. We have to get back to Earth soon, and I have to kill him. No, I *want* to kill him, for Ryan," I say, and I feel Mr Daniels kiss the top of my head.

"We will kill him for Ryan," Enzo says firmly, turning and locking those black eyes I love onto my own, showing me his resolution.

"I know," I say simply. I won't rest until my father pays for taking Ryan's life. The stone comes into view as we step back out of the forest, and it's bigger than I thought it was. It stretches into the sky, made of a pure white stone and it's smooth, with no visible marks on it. I look around, seeing nothing, and I have no clue where we should go from here.

"Let's spread out and search the area before the sun sets," Enzo suggests.

"I'm going to check out the stone," I say, stepping away from Mr Daniels. They walk off and start searching, while I walk straight up to the stone. I walk all the way around it, not spotting anything, and I place my hand on it, and it just feels cold. I pull the tube out of my pocket, pressing it to the stone and nothing happens.

"Great," I mutter, sitting down, and resting my head against the stone.

"*Mackenzie, Earth child,*" I hear a male voice whisper, making me jump, and look around. When the ground starts shaking, I freeze, and then it suddenly collapses in on itself. I fall straight down, not having any marks to help myself. Screaming so loud my throat hurts, I plummet down the hole in the ground. The drop feels endless as I continue to descend, with dirt hitting my face the entire time.

"Kenzie!" I hear Locke scream, seconds before my head hits something, and everything goes black.

Chapter 12

MACKENZIE

"*K*enzie!" A voice shouts my name, and I lift my head off the ground, holding my hand to my forehead where it throbs. I lift it away, feeling blood on my hand and everything is a little blurry. The room is pitch black except for little rays of light coming from dots in the ceiling where I fell, so I can't see much, but I remember someone shouting for me. At least I hope that was someone shouting to me.

"Hello! Anyone here?" I shout, coughing and forcing myself to sit up. Everything hurts, and I can't heal myself. I hate being this helpless. Blinking rapidly as blood drips into my right eye, I try to wipe it away, only to feel dirt from my hands sticking to the blood on my face. *Ugh.*

"Kenzie?!" I hear Locke shout from my right. Relief spreads through me, and I breathe out the long, nervous breath I was holding.

"I'm here, but I can't see anything!" I shout back. A small light comes into view, and then I can see Locke walking towards me, holding a make-shift flaming torch. It's really more of a stick with fire balancing on the end. Something that would spread easily if it wasn't for his fire mark. What I would give to have my fire mark in the darkness here. He rushes over when he sees me, falling to his knees, and putting the fire down next to us. It lights up the room, which is actually a tiny cavern and covered in bits of dirt and rocks.

"Shit," is all he says, placing his hand on my cheek, and I feel it start to warm up. I sigh as he heals me, the pain disappearing slowly from my body, and I sink my head into his hand.

"Is anyone else down here?" I ask, lifting my hand, and pushing some of the dirt out of his hair. He looks as bad as I do, but he doesn't seem to care. He only seems focused on me.

"I don't know. I saw you fall, and I ran and jumped in after you. This place is a maze though. Tunnel after tunnel that go around in circles by the looks of it," he tells me, and takes his hand away.

"Thank you for jumping in after me," I whisper, loving how sweet that was. He didn't think of his own life, he just jumped. I can't say I wouldn't do the same thing for him, because I would.

"I'd follow you anywhere, Kenz," he says, leaning closer and gently kissing me before pulling away, and standing up.

"I found a room, it's clean and has running water. We should camp there for the night, and hopefully, the others figure something out by morning. If nothing else, we should have some more natural light during the day," he says as he picks up the torch, and then leans back down for something else.

"This is yours," he offers me the silver tube, and I glare at it.

"I heard a weird voice when I was leaning against the stone holding that thing. I'm sure that tube is haunted or something," I say stubbornly, not wanting to take it. "I don't like ghosts."

"This might be part of the journey we need to make. You should still keep it," he responds, appearing serious and thoughtful. I'm not used to that from Locke, so I do as he asks. I put the tube into my pocket and take Locke's hand. We walk out from the small room we are in, and down a tunnel leading out from it. Locke leads me to the right, and we eventually come to a cosy room. It has a fire lit in the middle, a small bit of running water dripping down the one side of the wall. I can't see where the water is going or where it's coming from, but I'm grateful for it. I run over to it, washing my face and drinking some.

"Here," Locke comes over after putting the torch into the fire, and he has a small rag in his hands. He puts the rag in the water, and then presses it to my face. I let him slowly clean me, watching his eyes as he does.

"I love you Locke," I say, my voice echoing around the room. He pauses with the cloth on my cheek, and leans closer, lifting my chin with his finger.

"And I love you," he tells me, brushing his lips against mine in the most teasing way possible. He quickly pulls away when we hear the sound of foot-steps heading in our direction.

"You hear that?" he asks, and doesn't wait for my reply, as he stands in front of me, ready to defend me as a familiar face walks into the room.

"East!" I exclaim, stepping around Locke and wrapping my arms around him.

"Shit, I was fucking worried," East admits. I kiss

his cheek, looking behind him, but I don't see anyone else. "I came alone. When I heard Locke shout for you, I ran back and jumped straight in the hole. I don't know where Daniels, Logan and Enzo are," he answers my unasked question.

"They will find a safe way down," Locke says.

"That's not the problem. When I fell, I got caught on a branch and had a chance to look around. There are over ten different holes you can fall into, and all lead in different directions. If they came down after us, it may take them a while to find us," East explains, and I bite my lip. Crap, we could be lost down here for days, or even weeks.

"Don't panic, we will figure something out," Locke says and goes to sit in front of the fire. East pats my arm as he walks past, pulling his bag off and sitting next to Locke. I walk around the room, seeing nothing but the dirt walls and rocks on the floor. There really isn't much in here.

"Kenz, come here," Locke shouts from the other side of the room. I walk over, following his and East's gaze to look up at the ceiling near the water. There is a scratching noise, maybe sounding a little like something digging.

"Ariziadia must have its own wildlife. It could be a mole or something," I say, just as something breaks through the ceiling and falls to the floor. I look down at the black and white badger. It's cute as it shakes its head, then shimmers as it shifts back into Enzo.

"You're a badger," I gasp, covering my mouth with my hand.

"Good to see you too, Crowe. I've been digging and crawling for the last two damn hours, and I don't even get a hello?" he says grouchily, and I run straight into his arms. He catches me easily as I practically leap at him.

"I like badgers. They're cute," I say into his chest.

"Not another word, Crowe," he mutters.

"But maybe one day you can shift, and I can have a cuddle? That would be so cute," I say, chuckling as he kisses me. I suspect mostly just to shut me up.

"Don't push your luck," he replies quietly before pulling away and addressing East and Locke. "You haven't seen Logan or Daniels, have you? They jumped when I did, but this stupid place is a maze."

"I was just explaining that to Kenz and Locke," East answers.

"We don't know where they are," I say unhappily. I don't want us to be split up again while we're here. In this unfamiliar world, having my guys close is my only comfort. Plus, there's safety in numbers.

"I suppose I can dig through the walls of the tunnels and look for them?" Enzo offers, but I can tell he's exhausted.

"It can wait till you've had some rest," I begin, but he shakes his head.

"Will you get any sleep until you know they're safe?" he asks, and I consider lying, but I don't want to do that. Not to him. Not to any of them.

"Probably not," I admit begrudgingly. I feel terrible as I see the decision made on his face. "I'll go search for them. Those two can take care of you while I'm looking," he says.

"I don't need a babysitter," I mutter, not pleased.

"They're not fucking babysitters, Crowe. They're people who care about you, and right now, you're in a dangerous place and can't protect yourself. If someone you cared about was in danger, would you protect them?" he asks me, sounding even more drained. Instead of answering, I kiss him thoroughly and wrap my arms around him tightly. I can feel East and Locke's eyes on us, just as surely as I can feel Enzo's hands slide down my back to squeeze my ass. I chastise him with a quick nip to his earlobe once I pull away from his lips.

"If you get too tired, come back. Don't push yourself too far, and please stay safe," I instruct him seriously, and when he frowns, I use my finger to lift one side, then the other up. "Promise?" I ask.

"Promise. So long as *you* promise not to go anywhere without at least one of those two," he demands in return.

"I promise," I agree, stealing another kiss from him before he can leave. He steps back from me, and then shifts back into his cute badger, before darting back through the hole he came in.

"I never thought a badger would come in handy," East says, bringing my attention back to him and Locke.

"Who cares about practical, he's adorable," I reply with a smile.

"And my hawk isn't?"

"I think a hawk is meant to be more…majestic, is it?" Locke asks, but there's a sarcastic tone to his voice. East clearly doesn't notice it.

"Majestic tops cute, right?" he asks me, and I roll my eyes. *It's a good thing I love all my competitive guys. Whether they're majestic or cute.*

Chapter 13

MACKENZIE

_____

few hours have passed since Enzo went off to find the others, and I can feel the tension growing throughout my whole body. Why hasn't he found them yet? Or has he found them, but they've run into trouble?

"You okay, Kenz?" East asks from beside me. I shake my head and then burrow against his chest as he wraps his arms tightly around me and pulls me onto his lap. "They'll be fine," he whispers, rubbing his hands soothingly down my back.

"Then why are they taking so damn long?"

"Because this place is a maze," East answers quietly. I pull back to look into his eyes, watching the way they almost seem to flicker in the firelight. They seem to sharpen into focus with a sudden thought, and he lifts me off his lap, standing up. East's sudden movement wakes Locke, who'd been snoring on the other side of me.

"What's going on?" he grumbles, clearly unhappy at having been woken without an apparent reason.

"I'm going to go look for the others, and I have an idea to keep me from getting lost," East explains.

"And that idea is?" I prompt East, as Locke yawns and stretches.

"I can partially shift one of my hands into talons and mark the walls with them. Then, when I find the others, we can just follow the path back to you guys. Even if I don't find the others, I can find my way back to you two." East looks pretty impressed himself and his idea.

"How did we not think of that earlier?" Locke questions incredulously, clearly not as impressed with how long it took East to come up with it.

"I was tired, okay? It's not exactly been restful since we got here," East snaps.

"Hey! Chill out. I was only kidding," Locke replies, but I can see the strain taking effect on both of them. They really are spent. Hell, so am I.

"East, I think that's a great idea," I say quickly, hoping to avoid any more squabbles. I lean up and kiss him quickly. "But don't look for too long, I know you're tired. If you need to look, look, but hurry back," I add. He nods, leaning down to kiss me again before he leaves. I squeeze him tightly for a moment, so damn aware of the many things that could go wrong, but I also know I need to respect his choice here. "I love you, Easton Black," I whisper.

"Love you too, Kenz. Always," he replies, before walking to the edge of the entrance, and shifting his hand into a talon. I watch as he drags it along the wall he walks along.

"Wait!" I shout, and I see him freeze.

"Locke, can you make him a torch quickly?" I ask, and he nods, getting up and grabbing a stick, before using his mark to make a small controlled flame on the top. He passes it off to East, who nods in acknowledgement as he takes it.

"I'll see you both soon," he calls, and he heads down the tunnel again. I listen to the sounds of his talons on the wall until they disappear, leaving me and Locke sitting in silence.

"You look tense," Locke says gently, moving across the room to sit with me.

"I guess I am," I reply, still staring at the spot where I last saw East just moments ago.

"Take your shirt off," he suggests.

"Take my shirt off?" I echo in question, turning to face him with an eyebrow raised.

"Yeah, take your shirt off and turn back around," he answers. I shrug, not seeing why, but I do it anyway, slowly peeling off my shirt before setting it down in my lap. His hands are like ice as they touch my back, and I quickly realise his intention, just as his thumbs press down and glide down from my shoulder blades.

"You're giving me a massage? Is now really the best time?" I ask.

"It's never not a good time for any activity that involves you taking your shirt off, Kenzie," Locke replies in a low voice, as his hands trail lower down my back, his thumbs pressing down in circles over the knots under my skin. I can't hold back the moan that slips out my lips as he finds and works out all of the tense spots on my back. I find myself relaxing more and more as he carries on. His hands keep massaging, and I feel so comfortable, I don't even jump when he suddenly starts to hum. I don't recognise the tune, but whatever it is, it sounds good. Slow and deep. He shifts from humming to singing as he moves back up my back to rub my shoulders. The words make me smile as I listen.

Something about little Valentines always being there for each other and leading each other home.

"What song is that? Did you change some of the words?" I ask curiously, turning around to face him.

"I didn't change them. It's just a song my mum used to sing to me and Logan as kids. She has the most beautiful voice, but it's been a long time since I've heard it. Sometimes I just find myself humming or singing it for no reason. I guess it feels like home when I hear it, and since we're so far from home right now," he answers, tapering off. I find myself shocked at how much serious just came out of his lips at once.

"Why doesn't she sing anymore?" I ask.

"She hasn't sung since one of our dads died," he answers, his voice sounding suspiciously devoid of any emotion.

"I'm so sorry," I whisper, sliding my hands into his. His hands grip mine tightly back.

"It's been years," he says, as if that's meant to nullify any excuse for pain that he obviously feels about it.

"That doesn't matter," I say gently.

"I barely remember him to be honest, and it's not like I don't still have two other dads who are great. It's more what it did to my mum that upsets me," he replies in a thick voice. I hear him swallow as he tries to pull away to gain some composure, but I hold on tight to his hands, not letting him get away.

"It's okay," I murmur softly, releasing one hand so I can run it gently through his soft hair. "Do you want to tell me about it?" I probe lightly, not wanting to push, but I want him to know he can talk to me. He doesn't have to be ashamed of having feelings about it.

"She used to sing like that, every single day. She'd sing us to sleep, and when we'd wake up, she'd be singing and dancing around as she cooked breakfast. She was so bright. I don't mean intelligence bright, not that she's dumb, either. I just mean she had so much light in her. Her hair is blonde, even lighter than Kelly's, and our dads all call her sunshine. I always thought it was because of her hair, but it was just because of who she was." He takes a deep breath before continuing, and I wait, not wanting to rush him. "One day we woke up, and she wasn't in the kitchen singing, she was still lying in bed. Our dad had died a couple nights before, and she'd only just found out while we were sleeping. That's how it's been for years for now, no more singing, no more bright light. She's gotten a bit more like herself, mainly for me and Logan I think, but she's never been the same. Every day when I wake up in that house and it's silent, it feels like he's just died all over again. It feels like she died a little too," he finishes, resting his forehead against mine.

"It must be so hard for you and Logan. I'm so sorry," I finally reply quietly, squeezing his hands.

"It's okay. It's not like we had a horrible childhood like Enzo or anything. Our parents love both of us. It's just complicated," he says with a sigh.

"I know, but it doesn't take away your pain. Suffering isn't comparable," I respond, tilting his head up. "Thank you for sharing with me. Hopefully at some point, I can meet your family. You know, after we save the whole world," I tease.

"You and the others *are* my family. Of course you're all going to be meeting the rest of mine," he replies, smiling at me. I brush my hand across his cheek, before leaning in and kissing him softly, feeling his lips instantly respond to mine. He groans as he pulls me onto his lap, and my legs grip either side of his hips as his hands slide into my hair. It doesn't take long for us to rip our clothes off, and for Locke to slip inside of me.

"I love you," he whispers against my lips as he rocks in and out of me, making me moan. My moan echoes around the cave, but I don't really notice as I watch Locke.

"And I will always love you, no matter what," I reply and kiss him before he can respond.

Chapter 14

MACKENZIE

ackenzie Crowe. Mackenzie Crowe, it is your time. Come to me, Mackenzie Crowe…

I QUICKLY SIT up at the sound of a voice whispering to me. Everything seem hazy as I look around the cave and back down to Locke sleeping on the ground next to me. The fire is almost out, and the little amount of light in the room casts long shadows everywhere. I pull my clothes on, making sure to keep quiet so I don't wake Locke up.

MACKENZIE CROWE, grab your weapon and meet your fate…

I NEARLY JUMP as I hear the voice again. Looking around the empty cave, I wonder where the hell that voice is coming from. I glance at the silver tube on the floor, feeling a need to pick it up. Just as I do, the distant sound of music reaches my ears. It's a sweet, familiar I walk to the cave exit, looking back at Locke once before walking out. *I know I shouldn't just follow a disembodied voice, but I'm too curious not too.* Just outside the cave is a white orb of light, just floating in the air, lighting the whole tunnel up. I walk closer, feeling a little bit of warmth coming from it, and then it floats away slowly, straight down the tunnel.

FOLLOW. You must come alone for your marks. The test is yours alone to face or you will fail.

THIS TIME I don't jump when I hear the voice, but it still creeps me out. I don't know what to do. I bite my lip as I look back at the cave and then back towards the light. I know I shouldn't go far, especially not in this cave where I could get lost so quickly, but I want my marks back. I need them back, or this is all pointless. *I'm stronger than this. I can do this.* I repeat the sentences in my head as I walk down the straight part of the corridor, following the sound of the music, and the light orb. I look back, not seeing the warm light from the cave anymore, and I know I can't go back now without likely getting lost. The orb floats right in front of me, the music getting louder as we get closer to wherever it wants to take me. The orb floats into a large room at the end of the tunnel. The room is empty, just smooth white painted walls and dirt covered floor. The orb stops right in the middle, and I pause near it, turning and seeing the entrance I came through is has disappeared.

"What the hell?" I mutter, searching the room for another exit and seeing nothing but white walls.

"Weird ghost voice, now would be a good time for you to tell me what to do!" I shout, and my voice echoes around the room, but no one replies. I step back as the orb starts descending and hits the ground, spreading out into a circle of bright light.

STEP ONTO THE LIGHT. The light is all magic, all marked. It will decide your fate.

I PAUSE, glancing at the light as the voice whispers. Taking a deep breath, I remind myself the reasons why I need my marks back. Why I have no choice but to step into the light. My father has to die. Ryan needs revenge, and my men need me back with them. I can't just disappear and die here. I'm alone, and it frightens the hell out of me, but I must be strong on my own now. I step closer, placing one foot in the light circle and then the other. I wait, but nothing happens for a long time. Just silence, and then suddenly the light fades, and I fall to the floor in the dark room.

"Hello? What the hell was that?" I ask the weird voice, but nothing responds. I keep a tight grip on the silver tube as I stand up, looking around at the darkness, but I can't see a thing.

"Kennie," a deep voice says behind me, and I freeze. I can't move as I process the sound of that voice. A voice that both breaks my heart and fills me with a false sense of hope. I turn slowly, and almost can't believe the sight of Ryan standing not far from me. It's Ryan, but it's not. He is dressed in the clothes he died in, and blood covers his shirt and coat. His brown hair is messy, and he even has dirt mixed with blood on his right cheek. I remember my mum holding his cheek with her blood covered hand. A white light surrounds him, and he is almost see through. It's his spirit, his soul, but I don't have any marks to see his soul. This is impossible. I don't understand how he's here, and I don't know what to say as hot tears pour down my cheeks, so I just stare.

"I'm sorry," are the only words that escape my lips, and Ryan doesn't move. He is so still, so quiet. So…well, dead.

"Kelly. Kelly must know it was for her," he says each word slowly, his voice so distant, and his lips never move.

"She will know. I bet she already does. She knows you loved her, and she loves you," I say, harshly wiping my tears away. "I love you Ry, and I wish I could change what happened."

"You cannot change what was meant to be," his distant voice replies as I keep my eyes locked on his.

"Did it hurt? When you died?" I ask, needing to know if he suffered or not. Though I know if he says he did, it would break my heart even more.

"Not when you're loved, or when you're

remembered by those that loved you," he tells me, and it somewhat relieves me to know that.

"I miss you. I really, really do, Ry," I cry out, falling to my knees, and looking away from him.

"It's time for me to leave, for me to find peace. If you can face death, you're strong," Ry says, making me glance up, seeing him looking up at the ceiling.

"I'm not strong. I'm just a weak child who let her brother die," I sob out.

"If that is what you think, then join me in death," Ry says, looking back down at me and holding out an almost completely see through hand. "No more pain, and no more worry. You will have eternal peace." I stare at my brother's hand for a long time. The coward inside of me wants to accept it because it's the easy option, and it would mean I would get to be with my brother.

"No." I answer simply, standing up and shaking my head. "Life isn't easy, but I am needed here. If I die, it will be fighting to fix the mess I caused with my men at my side. I miss you Ry, and you have no idea how much I want to go with you, but I can't. I have to stay," I finally say, and he smiles.

"Kennie, I knew your answer, but I had to be the test. The next test will be based on your decision," he says and takes a step back. "Tell mum and our dads that I'm happy, and I miss them, won't you, Kennie?"

"I will," I say, trying not to sob anymore as he starts to fade away.

"Kennie, don't cry. I won't ever really leave. I love you too much," he says, and then he is gone, and I fall to the ground in tears.

Chapter 15

MACKENZIE

"Why are you sat there crying? Is seeing your brother not a gift?" A very familiar female voice whispers as I lift my head up and look around the empty, dark room.

"Hello?" I ask, wiping my tears away. No one replies, so I decide I might as well answer their question. "I'm crying because I miss him. He shouldn't have died so young, and especially not because of the decisions I made. I walked straight into the trap that killed him, and I wish I could change it." I answer honestly. It's something I never really wanted to admit out loud, but I feel better now I've said it.

"I guess we never want that. Yet, do you not think all death is fated? That we are all supposed to die at a certain time and date?" the voice replies to my left, but when I turn my head that way, I see nothing. But then again, it's so dark, I might not be able to see anyone anyway.

"No, I don't believe that. We have to have a choice, the ability to affect our own fate, or isn't it all pointless?" I reply, still searching for the owner of the voice and seeing nothing. This time I stand up, only holding the silver tube and feeling colder than I did before.

"I know that," the female voice laughs, sounding like she is standing right behind me. I spin around, seeing nothing. My heart races as my adrenaline surges from the feeling of fight or flight rushing over me. It's not like I really have the ability to fight without my marks, but there's nowhere to run either.

"Show yourself. No more games," I demand, and the voice laughs, echoing around the room.

"No games? Then what else shall we do?" she asks, almost innocently. She is still playing games, taunting me. I can hear it in her voice. I hear the slight movements of her feet in the room, but every time I turn, there doesn't look like there is anyone there. I know this adventure is meant to be a test, so maybe this is just another test. Ry was a test, but I don't know what for, and I have no idea what this one is about. If it is in fact a test, and not some crazy person who I happen to be in a cave with.

"You could help me leave here?" I suggest. I know she won't, I can feel it, but it's worth a shot. The guys have to getting worried about me now and have started to search.

"No one can leave here, not without their marks. You haven't earned yours yet, Mackenzie Crowe," she taunts, laughing once more. *Why does she sound so familiar to me?*

"How do I earn them?" I ask.

"By killing me," the voice says right in front of me, and then a figure slowly appears from nothing. Long black hair, wide blue eyes, torn clothes, and every feature I see in the mirror every single day. She's me. A version of me, anyway.

"How is this possible?" My eyes must be bulging as I look at her, at myself. She stands covered in her marks, more than I've ever possessed, and that's just from the glimpses of her skin that I can see. She's the me I want to be, so how can I kill her?

"There can only be one," she says, stepping towards me. Her hands are held out, facing down, and I feel the earth shake beneath our feet. I struggle for balance, as she stands there calmly. She stops using her earth mark and laughs. "This won't even be difficult, you're powerless," she comments snidely.

Powerless? I may have no marks, but I refuse to be called powerless by a freaking mirror image of me. A damn copy. A new feeling strikes me, not one of self-pity, or of fear, but determination. I will pass this test, there's no other option here. I couldn't save Ryan, but I will save myself, and everyone else that I care about. I won't lose anyone else, fate be damned if it has a plan for them. The other me smiles, as if she can hear my thoughts.

"I can. It's so cute you think you can beat me." She pulls back her dark hair and turns her head, pointing to a small mark just behind and slightly below her ear. It's one I've never seen before. It's like a basic eye design, but with elaborate curves coming off at the edges. "A mark that allows its possessor to read the thoughts of others," she says, running her fingers over it. "You could have had them all, but you were too weak. You lost what you had, and now you're nothing."

"You're wrong," I snap.

"How so? I mean look at you, unmarked, with no way to defend yourself. I could strike you down with a click of my fingers. Unless you give up now, I will become Mackenzie Crowe, and you will become nothing, just a shell that I walk in. I'll save your family, your men, and your friends for you, because we both know that you can't. Not without me."

"Shut up. You don't know me! You don't know what I'd do for them!" I shout, my voice echoing from the walls.

"Listen to me. Whatever it is, it wouldn't be enough, because *you* are not enough, Mackenzie Crowe."

"No, you listen to me, you half-assed imitation. I am the only Mackenzie Crowe. I will get my powers back, and I will get us home. And then, I'm going to make him pay for taking Ryan away, and stop him from hurting anyone else ever again!"

"Such confidence, and so unfounded," she says, and I feel the tube burning hot in my palm. I know it means something, it's with me for a reason.

Bring your weapon. The voice said bring your weapon, and I brought this. I run my thumb over the edges of it, feeling for a groove, a button, anything, but there's nothing.

"If you're so much stronger than me, then why are you asking me to give in? Why not just take my place?" I muse aloud, feeling the answers fall into place as I do. "You can't, can you?" I ask, narrowing my eyes on other me.

"I can do anything," she huffs.

"But you can't. You can't take me without my consent. You can't win. You're not stronger than me at all," I splutter, alarmed at my own conclusions. She laughs, moving towards me again, and I back away with each step she takes.

"I can't take you, but I *can* kill you. You're powerless to kill me though, aren't you?" she questions in a smug tone. Gods, I hope I never sound like that.

She jumps forward, and I dart out of the way, hitting and then rolling across the hard floor, holding in a pained groan from the impact. I reach for my powers by instinct, but none will answer me. The tube I cling to gets hotter. *Maybe…*

I call to the tube how I'd call to my powers, and almost drop it as it extends out into a spear, the pointed end darting out. So much power seems to flow through the metal, and I feel the waves of it roll up through my fingers, and up my arm, until it fills all of me with its energy. I point the spear at her, and she smiles.

"You're almost ready," she says with a smile,

and I nod. I know I am. I'm not powerless, and I never will be. With or without my marks, I can still fight. I strike her quickly, watching her fade away around the spear in her chest. "Just one more test," her voice finishes, leaving me alone in the room.

Chapter 16

MACKENZIE

he floor suddenly cracks, and I tumble downward, even deeper into the ground than I thought possible. I brace myself for a hard impact, but I fall into water instead. As soon as I hit the water, I try to swim back up, but something keeps puling me down. I know where I am the second I submerge into the water. I've reached the Zarrci Honzel.

I try to hold my breath, as I struggle to break free of whatever grip is holding me down, but there's no use. My mouth flies open as I gape for air. I wait for the water to rush into my mouth, for myself to suffocate, but it doesn't happen. I don't drown as I float under the water. Something is allowing me to breathe. I notice I can hear something from below me, whispered words. I swim down towards them, trying to hear what is being said to me. Finally, I am close enough to make them out, but I wish I wasn't.

"Mackenzie, you are willing to fight, and you are brave enough to stand even without your marks, but are you brave enough to die?" the voice asks me.

"You want me to die?"

"I want nothing outside of this water, and in here I seek nothing but your truth." It answers vaguely.

"What's that supposed to mean?" I groan, my head hurting from all the things I've had to process in such a short time.

"I will show you what may await you if you leave here with your marks returned, and then you will give me your answer." Before I can agree or disagree with that statement, I'm drawn into blackness.

I WATCH as I strike him, just as he strikes me, and then we both go down. All my powers weren't enough to save me. I can't control my movements here, only watch on through my eyes as I fall to the floor.

My father stands back up, and I know my strike missed. I failed.

My mum breaks free of her captors' hold just as my eyes find her. She rushes at him, and the full force of her powers hits him at once. She slams him back into the far wall with her air mark and uses it to then manipulate the air around us to pull the spear to her. She holds it in her hand, and fury shines in her eyes as she deals the final blow, killing Alaric and ending this all.

She runs to me, but it's too late. She falls to the floor, sobbing at my side uncontrollably as the last of my life fades away.

"THAT CAN'T BE REAL. I refuse to believe you!" I snap at the Hoznel as I come back into the water, and away from the vision.

"You can pretend that you refuse to believe, Mackenzie Crowe, but you know you cannot deny you saw a truth. I showed you my truth, now give me yours. Are you willing to die if it means the marked will be at peace? If it means saving everyone else?" it asks me.

Would I be willing to die for marked peace? I don't know. But I do know, I would die for my family, for my guys, and for my friends. I would die if they would all be able to find peace from it.

"I would die for them, if that's what it takes, but…"

"You have a condition?"

"No. I would die for them, but I don't accept that it's the only way this can go. I can't accept that. I will go, and I will fight, whether you give me my marks or not. If I must, I will die for them, but I will not give up and go gently," I answer defiantly.

"You must never simply give up. You must be willing to fight, but also willing to die. If you're giving up, you're not willing to fight," it responds. The grip pulling me down leaves me, and I suddenly feel the urge to swim for air. I know I can't open my mouth again to ask it anything more. *Does that mean I pass? Or have I failed?*

There's no time to dwell on that, however, as I swim up to escape the water before I drown. I break through the surface, and feel my skin start to burn. My marks flare back into existence all over my body. I float on my back in the water as it happens. I count them as they begin to form. More marks than I ever possessed before pop up. I smile as I feel a mark flare behind my ear. Reading minds could be fun. Once the burning has stopped, I've lost count of the marks I now possess. I turn over in the water and swim for the edge of the natural pool, heaving myself out of the water.

I lie on my back as soon as I get onto ground, and take deep, panting breaths. I hear someone cough beside me, as if coughing up water. I quickly turn, ready to face off anyone who could be here to hurt me, but I freeze when I see Enzo lying there, drenched. I rush to him, holding my hands over his chest as I'm ready to heal him, but I freeze, noticing something strange.

His skin is covered in new marks too. I know immediately, the Honzel didn't just test me, it split us all up for a reason. It wanted to test all of us, separately. I run my fingers over a new mark he has on his neck, and his dark eyes fly open.

"Crowe," he mutters.

"I'm here. What did it show you?" I ask nervously, wondering if our tests had been the same.

"My father at first. And then it showed my sister dying. We need to get back to the academy before it's too late. She's going to die if we don't," he says urgently, sitting up.

"We have to wait for the others first. But I

promise, we will go to try and save her," I say, slipping my hands into his and squeezing them tightly.

"What do you mean we have to wait for the others?" he asks, and I point at the water.

"I think they're all under, being tested to see if they're worthy of their marks," I explain, biting my lip nervously as I glance the water. I wonder what's taking them all so long.

"But I thought this was just for you? We already have our marks, why would we be tested?" Enzo asks. I lift his hand up, having spotted a new mark on his hand too.

"Look," I say gently, holding his hand at an angle so he can see the lightning-shaped mark on his hand.

"I have new marks." He looks at them in shock, before pulling his hands away and taking off his shirt. I can't help but run my eyes all over him heatedly, remembering the last time we were underground in a cave like this one.

"There are so many," I whisper, running my fingers over each of the marks that grace his skin.

"If you move your hand any lower, Crowe," he all but growls at me, and I laugh.

"We shouldn't. We need to be here for the

others when they get out. Who knows what any of them had to see," I say, trying to reason.

"Fine, you're right," he says, but he pulls me down to him, and hungrily crashes his lips against mine anyway. His hands clench at my body roughly, pulling me against him. I return the kiss, sense leaving me quickly, but then he pulls away. "I had to do that at the very least," he explains when he sees my expression. I'm about to reply, when I see East emerge from the water. His eyes seem to find us instantly, but he's unable to swim to us just yet. We watch on quietly as he's blessed with new marks.

I'm almost relieved at seeing him, but I already knew East would be worthy. All my guys are. It's just a waiting game for them to finish their tests and join us, so we can return to Earth and face my father, finishing our biggest test together.

Chapter 17

MACKENZIE

"It's been too long," I say, pacing up and down the rocky ground outside the pool. Logan, Locke and East all came out of the water with new marks ages ago, but Mr Daniels is nowhere to be seen. I glance over at Locke who is still shaking the water out of his hair.

"He might have just fallen in later than we did," East says, standing close to me and watching me pace. I know he is worried too.

"It doesn't make sense," I shake my head, and continue stomping back and forth. I'm a few steps away from jumping in the water and asking it where the hell he is.

"Or he failed his test because of his past. He

has more demons than most," East points out quietly.

"He will pass," I snap at East as I stop to glare at him. When he holds his hands up in surrender, I realise how harsh that sounded. I know it's not East's fault. East watches me, waiting for me to calm down before he comes over to me. I sigh, rubbing my face, "I'm sorry I snapped. I know what you're saying. I just can't allow myself to think like that or I'm going to lose it."

"I shouldn't have even said it. The test messed me with me, and I'm just feeling a little off," East admits, and I wrap my arms around his waist, watching the water.

"The test messed with me too. It messed with us all," I say, glancing quickly at Enzo and the twins. They're resting their backs against a wall and watching the water with dazed expressions. They all look lost in their own thoughts. What ever happened to them in the water, it has shaken them much like it has me.

"What did you see?" he asks me.

"Ry," I say quietly, leaving out the part about myself. "His soul, spirit, or whatever you believe it is."

"His soul. I knew he would stick around to say goodbye," East says gently.

"It broke my heart, both what he said and seeing him leave once again," I admit, not fully over it.

"Ry is at peace," East tells me gently and I nod, resting my head against his chest and continue to watch the still water. I don't know how long I stare until I see a bubble pop against the surface, and then another, just seconds before Mr Daniels bursts out the water. Mr Daniels eyes lock with mine as I break away from East and watch him receive his marks. I see two marks appear on his cheeks, looking like hands, and a mark on his forehead which is shaped like angel wings. *What the hell are those?*

"Finally," Enzo comments, stepping up to my other side as Mr Daniels finally gets all his marks and starts swimming over to us. Enzo and East grab his arms, pulling him onto the ground as he coughs up water and lies on his back as I kneel next to him. I spot marks on his hands, and the one behind his ear like we all have.

"You okay?" I ask when he stops coughing water and sits up. He immediately pulls me to his chest and kisses the top of my head.

"Yes, but we need to get home right now. They are going to kill your dads, Enzo's sister, and anyone that doesn't side with your father. I saw it," Mr Daniels tells me, his worried tone tells me all I need to know.

"What about my mother?" I ask as I stand up, and Enzo offers a hand to help Mr Daniels up.

"I didn't see her," he says.

"He will keep her alive. She isn't dead yet," I say firmly. If the vision I was shown is true, then she will be the one that kills him. I'm almost happy it's her. It's the perfect revenge for Ryan, well, only if I don't die next.

"We need to leave," Locke says, and we all don't say a word as we agree. My twelfth mark starts warming up on my neck, just like the tube heated up to tell me to use it before. I have new gifts, and I'm stronger now…so maybe I can control a portal?

"I have an idea," I say, stepping away from them all.

"What?" Logan asks.

"Just stay back, in case this goes wrong," I warn them, but I hear them all take a step forward to stand right behind me. Typical, stubborn ass men. I mentally pray this works. Closing my eyes, I picture Kelly as I hold both my hands out in front of me and call my twelfth mark. Nothing happens for a while, and I frown, opening my eyes again as I lower my arms.

"I thought I could open a portal to Kelly, but nothing happened," I turn and explain to my guys.

"Alaric said the twelfth mark was connected to emotions. Even though he used great emotional *pain* to activate it, love could work just as well now that you're stronger. Try thinking about how much you love Kelly," Mr Daniels suggests, and I nod, facing forward once again and lifting my arms. I picture when I first met Kelly, a day that seems like almost yesterday, even though we were only eight. Kelly and her parents had just moved into the empty house on our street, and I was dragged by my mum to say hello. Kelly ran out the door once we knocked, holding a giant cookie in her hand, and I could hear her mum shouting at her to come back. She asked me if I wanted to share the cookie, but we had to hide. Since then I loved that girl like a sister. I open my eyes as my twelfth mark burns the back of my neck, and a blue shining portal has opened in front of me. The inside is mainly blue glowing swirls, and what looks like a plain stone room is on the other side.

"It worked," I say, breathlessly, tilting my head

to the others as they step closer.

"Let's see where it goes then," Locke grins, before walking straight into the portal. Logan goes in next, with a wink in my direction. East follows, and then Enzo, and I look over at Mr Daniels who watches the water. Mr Daniels kneels down, placing his hand on the ground.

"Thank you for the treasured moments with my sister, and for my new gifts. We will destroy the evil that is coming to your world. I promise you that," he says firmly, making me wonder what happened when he was under the water. He eventually straightens up and nods once at me before walking into the portal. I walk through last, feeling the cold wash of the portal surround my body. It makes me feel like I can't breathe until I get through the other side, and I walk into the small room behind my silent guys. They move out the way, so I can see Kelly, fast asleep on a small bed. There isn't much in the room, just the bed, a small dresser and a rug on the floor.

"Can you all wait outside? I need to talk to Kelly alone about something," I whisper. Enzo kisses my forehead before walking to the door, and the others all follow him out, shutting the door behind them.

Chapter 18

MACKENZIE

"Kells?" I whisper, walking over and touching her shoulder gently as I sit on the edge of her bed. She blinks her eyes open. She looks exhausted, even as she wakes up, with bags under her eyes, pale skin and messy hair. It's like she has just given up, and I'm not having that. I'm not losing my best friend.

"You're back sooner than I thought. I saw it, but it was unlikely," she tells me, more muttering to herself as she sits up on the bed. "There is a towel just under the bed where you have sat." I smile, reaching under the bed and grabbing the blue woven towel, wrapping it around my shoulders. My wet hair still drips down my back, but at least I'm not cold anymore.

"Thanks," I mutter, watching her closely as she looks down at her hands and starts rolling the silver ring on her thumb around in circles. I've seen the ring before, but never on her. It was Ryan's. My parents gave it to Ryan as a present when he finished The Marked Academy. I almost break down in tears at seeing her wearing it, because I know he must have given it to her before he died. They were going to be together. They loved each other, and now there is only a message from the dead left between them.

"Tell me..." she finally says, but she doesn't look at me as she speaks.

"You know I spoke to Ryan?" I ask her, needing to make sure we are talking about the same thing.

"I saw you talking with him. I felt your emotion and pain in the vision. I just couldn't hear what you spoke about," she admits and finally looks up at me with emotion filled eyes and tears streaming down her cheeks.

"Ry..." my voice cracks, and I have to clear my throat as I grab her hand. I expect her to pull away from me, but she doesn't. "Ry, he told me to tell you that he died for you. I knew he did from the moment he volunteered, but I don't think you knew because you were so out of it. He knew you would die if he didn't step in. It was you or him, and he chose you." I can't help but pull Kelly into my arms as she sobs, great heaving sobs that feel like they could crush me.

"I miss him so, so, damn much, Kenz. I don't know how to keep fighting without him, without the promise of a future with him at my side," she admits, and I pull back, holding her shoulders with my hands and making her look at me.

"You fight because he would want that. He would want you to live, to be happy, and to fall in love again. You fight so that he didn't die for nothing," I tell her, and she nods, wiping her face with her other hand.

"I won't love again, it will always be Ry for me," she says sadly as I rub a finger over the ring, getting her attention. "He gave me this and told me we would be forever. He wanted to marry me and have kids. All the normal stuff. We even joked that Auntie Kenzie would be getting our kids into trouble all the time."

"I'm so sorry," I say honestly, I can't even imagine losing one of my guys. I imagine all of us having a future together, and to lose it is impossible to fathom unless it's happened to you.

"So, when I say he was everything to me, I

mean it. He was my only future on Earth," she says firmly.

"You don't know *everything*, oh great seer," I tease her, and she laughs.

"I kinda do," she admits, tapping a finger against her head, and now it's my turn to laugh.

"Now, do you have any spare clothes, and maybe some way to wash our faces? We are both ugly criers, and we have to leave this room at some point,"

"Speak for yourself," she jokes, as I get up off the bed, and she follows me. "I've got clothes for you and all your guys in the bathroom. I told you I see everything," she says, showing me into the hidden door almost behind the bed, that opens up into a bathroom of sorts. It's all pretty basic, with stone counters and water held in a cut-out sink. There are six piles of clothes on the floor by the door, and Kelly picks one up.

"Yours," she says as she hands them to me.

"Thanks, Kells. I meant what I said. He really would want you to find love again, when you're ready. Please don't count yourself out just yet," I say, and immediately feel a little bad when I see the tears well in her eyes again. Did I push her too far?

"Oh no, I know that look, Kenzie Crowe," Kelly

says firmly. "You are not to feel bad for my tears. Alaric caused my pain, not you. Now clean yourself up, I have to speak to King Elnam before we leave. He's under the impression he will be sending some guards to escort us, but they're really not necessary," she adds, heading for the door.

"Wait, is it the dragon shifting guys he wants to send with us? Taelon?" I ask curiously, and Kelly turns sharply, giving me weird look.

"Why would you ask that!?" she demands.

"Just curious. Gods, Kells, relax. They seem okay, for Ariziadian marked anyway," I respond with a shrug.

"I don't think they should come is all," Kelly says firmly, her mind clearly made up.

"Okay then, whatever you say, oh great seer," I say jokingly, rolling my eyes as I make a beeline for the hot water to clean up. I hear her footsteps as she all but runs out the door. *I wonder what that was about?*

"Is it okay to come in?" Logan shouts from outside Kelly's room.

"Sure!" I call back, before splashing some water over my face.

"Any reason you're using a sink to clean up when there's a bathing pool over there?" Logan asks, as he steps into the room. I turn in his direction and follow the his outstretched hand to the pool dug into the floor of the room that I'd completely missed. I didn't think to look at the floor in the corner of the room, I guess. He doesn't waste any time whatsoever, stripping off his clothes and jumping in. I shrug, deciding I might as well join him, there's plenty of room. I shimmy out of my torn and dirty clothing, leaving them discarded on the floor, as I cross to Logan, dropping into the pool of hot water beside him. I sigh, as I feel the heat relaxing all the tension across my body.

I barely notice one of the others sliding into the pool, followed by another, until they're all squished in here with me. None of them seem the slightest bothered by the others, just content to be here with me, and I smile. *Gods, I love my guys.*

"We love you too, Kenz," East's voice says, and I turn to look at him accusingly. He smiles sheepishly, before showing me is telepathy mark.

"Try and keep out my mind, Easton Black. Or I'll start delving into yours," I threaten, winking at him.

"You can fucking read minds now?" Locke exclaims, giving East a perturbed look.

"Yes, and can I just say, I have never met anyone else who thinks about burgers so much," East says, giving him a knowing look. I look between the two of them in confusion, just as Locke bursts out laughing

"Shut it, mate," he finally says, once he stops himself from laughing. I just roll my eyes, happy to leave them to whatever joke they have between themselves. I lean back against the huge bath's edge and rest my head.

I feel a hand grip mine, and open one eye to peek at who it is. Enzo is looking at me, clearly worried about everything going on, but content to enjoy this short moment of peace together. I savour it, worried that it may be our last.

If this is our last peaceful moment, all six of us together, then I would damn well enjoy it while I can.

Chapter 19

MACKENZIE

"*A*gain, I have to say, I don't think they should be coming with us," Kelly insists, but King Elnam isn't listening to her at all. He'd already said, several times, that he wouldn't put his full trust in Earth's marked, and that he wanted an Ariziadian presence. He said it was both in case we needed the support, but also to report back to him on what happens and about our world itself. I guess meeting us has made him curious.

"I have a parting gift for you, Mackenzie Crowe," King Elnam says, pulling out a small, old book from inside his cloak. He holds it out for me, and I take it as he explains. "It is a book with all the marks we know about. All of you have received more marks than the usual twelve your kind are used to receiving, therefore you will need to learn about these new marks."

"Thank you, this means a lot," I say honestly, handing the book to Locke to put it in the bag he has.

"I hope you take this gift as a sign of trust, with hope we can build a future between Earth and Ariziadian marked one day. Since you returned with so many marks, the other clan leaders and I have spoken in great detail, and we have decided to count Earth marked as another clan. We offer our alliance, and our help if you should need it," he tells us all, and I'm honestly shocked into silence.

"We have councils of leaders, and we will discuss this with them once the war is over. I can speak for the London council, of which I am a member, and accept this alliance," Mr Daniels says, offering his hand. King Elnam slides his hand up Mr Daniels' arm, so they shake elbows more than hands before Mr Daniels steps back.

"I still believe we don't need any guards with us," Kelly chimes in again.

"Just leave it, Kells. We can't waste any more time arguing," I say, and she nods.

"You're right, and we need to go now if we're going to do this in time," she agrees. "Portal it up, oh mighty chosen one," Kelly says, holding out her hands dramatically, making me smile as I try and hold back a laugh.

"Thank you for your assistance, King Elnam. I will do whatever it takes to stop my father," I promise to the king, and he nods. My eyes catch on Taelon, and I notice that he's glaring at Kelly. *Did something happen between them while we were at the Honzel? Is that why she doesn't want them coming with us? Do they not get along?* A part of me is a little tempted to dip into her mind and find out, but I know it's none of my business. She'd tell me if she wanted me to know. I internally sigh, deciding to leave it for now.

"I hope you are successful in your endeavour, Mackenzie Crowe. I also hope you will not need to fall back into my world again. Your first portal was quite destructive, so I can only hope that your skills have improved for your journey home," he responds, and I try not to roll my eyes. I hadn't seen any signs of destruction. "Not everything can be seen with your eyes, child," he snaps, clearly having read my mind.

"I'm sorry, it was just a thought. I didn't mean to offend. Thank you for your generosity and allowing us to stay in your world unharmed until we could return home. We will offer the same courtesy to our guests," I say, nodding towards the dragon guard he's sending with us. He nods, accepting my words.

"I wish you luck then, all of you," he says finally, and I smile, stepping away to make our portal home.

To get us home, I think about my dads, and how much I love them. My real dads, the one who raised and loved me. I feel the portal coming into form and relax.

"Are you all ready?" I ask, and the guys nod confidently, having travelled through two portals now. Kelly grabs my hand, and I grip hers back, figuring she must be nervous. The Ariziadian marked all look nervous, but not to be shown up by our confidence, they stride through the portal first. I walk forward to pass through with Kelly next, allowing the guys to bring up the rear.

Now is the time. I will save everyone from my father, or I will die trying. The vision the Honzel gave me flashes in my mind; me dying, and my mum being the one to finish this, killing my father. I grip the spear in my other hand tighter. I'd called it out of the water before we'd stepped through the portal to get back to Kelly. I figured since it was in the vision, it was important, and so I wasn't about to leave it behind.

Kelly squeezes my hand, just as we step into the blue shimmer, and then we fall back through the portal, into our home world.

Chapter 20

MACKENZIE

"What are you all doing here?" I hear Dad M ask in shock, and I begin to push through my guys and the guards, with Kelly at my side. I hear the rattle of chains moving just as my dads come into view. Enzo's sister, a bunch of teachers, and some people I don't know are all chained to the wall with them. Dad M is the only one awake out of the lot, leading me to believe they must be drugged or something.

"Dad!" I shout, running over to Dad M and throwing my arms around his neck, despite the fact he can't hug me back as he's restrained. When I pull away I can see his relief. I can also see that he looks awful, and a quick glance around the room shows everyone else appears much the same way. Dirty, tired, and not in a good state at all.

"I thought you were gone, thought I'd lost you," he says, kissing my forehead as I lift his chained arms to see the marked handcuffs on his wrists.

"Why aren't they waking up?" Enzo demands after trying to wake his sister and failing.

"They inject us with something every day, so I don't know why I'm awake. Maybe they messed up and gave me a lower dose," my dad answers.

"You can heal them," Taelon tells Mr Daniels, looking intently at the marks on his cheeks.

"What? How?" Mr Daniels asks.

"The marks on your cheeks are extended healing gifts. They don't work like the normal healing mark. They can only heal poison or deadly bites. Back on Ariziadia, those marks are very useful and highly regarded," he explains.

"Let's give it a try then," Mr Daniels says, walking over to Enzo's sister and placing his hands on her face. Mr Daniels closes his eyes, the marks on his cheeks lighting up brightly, and then Stacey's eyes pop open with a gasp.

"You're alive! They told everyone you were dead," Stacey cries as Enzo hugs her. We all happily watch as they hold each other and then Stacey's eyes meet mine.

"You need to stop him, he's destroying everything," she says.

"What has Alaric done so far?" I ask, almost not wanting to hear the answer. Mr Daniels heals Dad P as Stacey explains.

"He has killed the entire London council, the New York council, and the Paris council. He must be close to getting the last two, but they've hidden from him so far," she says, and there is a horrified silence in the room as we all process this.

"Fuck," Locke breathes out what we are all thinking.

"The London council is not destroyed. It has me, and I'm officially making Kenzie, Kelly, the twins, East, and Enzo new council members, until we have destroyed Alaric and we can have a vote," Mr Daniels says firmly, pulling his hands away from Dad P as he groggily wakes up. He looks straight at me, so much relief in his eyes.

"Come here, Kennie," he tells me, and I run over to him, holding him close as I feel him kiss my forehead. "I knew you weren't gone. No one beats my little Kennie that easily."

"So, council members, what are we going to do now?" Stacey asks, and none of us have a reply. Other than the intention to kill Alaric, we are pretty much winging this.

"Also, the marks on your hands can open any lock. Like these handcuffs," Taelon tells us.

"Daniels, you focus on waking everyone up, and the ones with the locking breaking mark, you start unlocking everyone," East says. We all get to work, and I hold my hands over my Dad's handcuffs, thinking of the mark on my hand. The mark lights up with a slight burning sensation for a second, but then his handcuffs fall to the ground and I'm pulled into my dad's arms. We all make quick work of releasing everyone and just have to wait for Mr Daniels to wake up Dad L and everyone else.

We find that most are either old teachers of Marked Academy, or family of the council members that were killed. We're in a large warehouse, surrounded by boxes, and I bet there are rebel guards outside. *I wonder if I could just create a portal to get everyone out of here without them even noticing?*

"Nope, it's too much power, and we need to make a solid plan of attack, rather than just jumping in. We were lucky there are no guards inside here when we came through," East says, clearing reading my mind again, but I don't argue with him. He's right. Though, I am annoyed at his new tendency to just pop into my mind whenever he likes. We're going to have to discuss that later.

"First off, where is Alaric?" I ask everyone that is awake, and it's Dad P that answers.

"He has control over the academy, and it's his base of operations. If he's anywhere, it's there."

"With your mum," Dad M points out with a slight growl.

"We need to get close, but it has to be some-where he wouldn't expect. We have the element of surprise for now, and we can't lose that. It's our only chance to end this. Does anyone have any ideas? It's not like we can sneak up on an island; he'd see us coming a mile away," Enzo points out, speaking to the room. A woman puts her hand up, standing up shakily with a nervous expression when I nod to her.

"My name is Linda. I went to school with Alaric, and I was also a teacher there for many years. I have a house on the mainland. It's just across the water from the academy, as I didn't want to live in there," she begins, and I listen impatiently for how this will help us. "It has an underwater tunnel in the basement that leads into the Academy's basement. No one else knows it's there. It's an old tunnel, and I'm warning you now that it's probably falling apart from lack of use and upkeep. It will likely be dangerous," she explains quickly, probably noticing my expression. I give her a small smile, hoping to make up for my impatience.

"Even falling apart, I still think it's the better option than just walking straight into the academy randomly," I state, and there are mumbled agreements. "Okay, so we're using the tunnel, then. I guess there's only one more thing I need to ask; who's coming with us?" I say, looking around at all of them. They aren't in a good state, not to fight anyway, exhausted from their torture, and unable to be completely healed without the time and manpower to do so. I'm not going to force them if they don't want to do this. I'm surprised when nearly everyone in the room, bar one or two, puts their hands up.

"We have all lost someone to Alaric and his rebels, and we will fight to get our revenge," Linda says firmly, and I totally understand that.

"I promise you will get your revenge. Alaric *will* die," I say, leaving out the fact that the price of his death will likely be my life.

"Alright, let's go. We can knock out the guards, and grab their keys. They must have cars around here somewhere," Mr Daniels suggests, and none of us say another word as we walk to the door. We all know, one way or another, this ends tonight.

Chapter 21

MACKENZIE

*CW*e drive in silence, well, mostly. The only sounds come from Locke attempting to break the tension with an inappropriate joke as we get caught at a traffic light. Nobody even pretends to force a laugh, though, blanketing us all back into silence.

The tension in the cramped car makes me feel like we're heading to a funeral. It reminds me of the only funeral I've ever attended, the one for Dad L's sister Ria. The solemn mood of that day is practically echoed in the car, and I can't help but think it's fitting, considering I could be heading to my death right now. I must have been too young to remember Alaric's funeral, considering he was gone before I was old enough to even remember him. I wonder if it felt like this too. Thinking of him making them all go through that when he was alive the whole time, it makes me even more furious. Just another hurt he's caused my family to add to the list of his crimes.

As much as I'm trying to stay positive, to cling onto hope that I will make it through this alive and the Honzel was merely testing me, I felt the truth in that vision. I felt the realness of my potential demise. It needed to know I was willing to risk it all, because that's what it may require. I'm risking my life, my future with the guys, all to save everyone I care about, and to make sure they get the futures they deserve. This is more than just revenge for what he's done to me, or for what he did by killing Ryan, it's giving peace to everyone.

We finally reach Linda's house, and some of the others' cars are already parked outside. We're all parked sloppily, nobody caring enough to straighten up right now. *We might not even make it back after all, so, why should any of us care?*

We file into Linda's home, gathering in the open plan dining and living room while we wait for the last of those coming with us. I feel eyes on me and turn to look for the source, finding East watching me with a concerned look on his face. I force myself to smile at him, but he won't meet my eyes as he turns away.

"I just need to talk to East a minute, keep an eye on things for me," I whisper to Enzo, who's standing next to me stiffly. He nods, grazing his hand across my cheek before I squeeze past him and head over to East.

I grab East's hand, leading him upstairs and out of the way of prying eyes so we can talk privately. I push open the first door we reach, and find a blandly decorated room, with no real personal items in here. A guest room, I'd guess. I pull East in there with me, shutting the door behind us.

"What was that about?" I ask him directly. We don't have time to skirt around the subject.

"You're not going," East states, stepping closer. I hear a metallic jingle, and my eyes latch onto the marked handcuffs in his hands. He must have swiped them from the warehouse after we rescued everyone. I step back from him nervously, putting my hands up in a stay back gesture.

"Now isn't the time to get kinky, East," I joke lamely, not even garnering a smile from him.

"Don't make jokes, Kenz. How can you even think of making fucking jokes when you're walking to your death?" he shouts, his voice sounding both pained and pissed off all at once. Shock washes over me like someone's drenched me in a bucket of ice water.

"What do you mean?" I question innocently, though my response is a few seconds too late. The lie in my words shattering any peace between us.

"You know what, Kenzie. I heard you in the car, what you were thinking…you know you'll die trying to stop him and you're still willing to go there? Well, *I'm* not willing to let you go, willing to lose you. I'm sure the others will agree with me about you staying here once I fill them in." He looks almost regretful as he quickly snags my wrist before I can even blink, and slaps the first cuff onto my wrist. "I'm sorry, but I know you won't stay by choice."

"I'm sorry too, East," I whisper, blinking back the tears that are threatening to fall. He doesn't want me to die, I know that. How can I be mad at his actions right now, when I know I'd do the exact same thing? I can't let him do this though, there's just too much at stake here.

"For what?" he asks, and I bite my lip, leaning up as if to whisper in his ear. Instead, I slip free from the cuffs that he hasn't activated yet and slip it over his wrist instead, snapping the other end to the headboard of the bed. I use my protection mark to activate the cuffs quickly, not making his same mistake of waiting too long.

"For that," I answer in a subdued voice. Stepping back, I look away from the accusing look on his face.

"Let me go, Kenz!" he snaps. "If you don't uncuff me right now, I'll shout for the others," he says in a determined voice, and I know he would. I can't risk that happening, as I know they'd side with him on this.

"I'm sorry, East," I apologise again, and use one of my new marks as I place my hand on his cheek. His body flops as he hits the floor, instantly unconscious from my touch. I flinch at the loud noise it makes, worried, both in case I hurt him, and that someone heard it. I watch the door silently for a few moments, half expecting someone to barge in here and find out what I've just done. When minutes pass with no intrusion, I let out a breath and crouch down beside him. "I really am sorry," I whisper, before laying a kiss on his lips gently, and pulling away to look at his face. I commit every last detail to my memory, the shape of his lips, the way the natural highlights in his hair catch the light, the sharp edges of his cheekbones and jaw. The way I look at him now feels a little like how you see someone important to you for the first time. It's special, a defined moment. It's not like the millions of other times my eyes have run over him, as I know that this could be the very last time I see him. My heart feels like breaking as I stand up, heading for the door.

As I leave, I fight the urge to say a goodbye. Saying goodbye would mean I've given up, and I'm not quite ready to do that yet. I decide right there that this won't be the last time I look at that stupidly perfect face of East's. I swear it to myself, and to him, as he lies there unconscious on the floor and chained to a stranger's bed, unable to follow. Then, I turn and head to walk into the fire, without him by my side.

Chapter 22

MACKENZIE

"Where's East?" Enzo asks me when I join them downstairs. I notice that most of the people that were here have already headed down to the basement, and only Enzo and Logan are left waiting for me. I feel waves of guilt slam into me, and I swallow thickly.

"He's decided to stay here," I lie. I hate the words even as I say them. Lying has never been something I've been comfortable doing, but to save everyone, I'm willing to cross the line.

"No fucking way," Enzo snaps.

"He wouldn't, no. We need to talk some sense into him," Logan says, looking frantically at the stairs, before taking a step in their direction. I move into his way, blocking him and Enzo from storming up there.

"I get it, really. I couldn't believe it either," I say softly. "But we do not have the time to go convincing East to come with us, and I won't forgive either of you if you forced him there. We need to leave, now." Neither of them looks happy at my proclamation, but they appear to accept it as they seem to deflate in front of me. I see Daniels watching me and the others from the kitchen, overhearing our argument. I don't know why, but I feel like Daniels knows I'm lying. I can see it in his eyes, but he looks away before I can make sure he believes me. At least no one has gone upstairs.

"This way," Stacey holds open a door in the kitchen, and we all look to her from the dining room. She steps in, pauses and looks back at us. "You can all swim, right? Or have the water and air marks?"

"Why?" I ask, pushing through the twins, and stopping next to Daniels who is watching Stacey curiously.

"Okay, so when describing the tunnel layout, Linda explained to me the reason the tunnels aren't used anymore. They are completely flooded and

have been for years. There's a hole in there some-
where, because fish and stuff are in there," she says.

"How did you use them to get to school then?"
Daniels asks Linda, who is hovering back behind
the rest of us.

"By being smart, and the air mark is my most
powerful mark. I make a bubble of air around
myself and use my water mark to push the bubble
through the tunnels. I did it countless times and
never had a problem. The bubble scares off the
fish, so they weren't an issue," she explains, and
there's a long silence as we all think about it. Crap,
this just got a lot more complicated, but it can't stop
us. Luckily, most of us have both the air and water
mark; they're the most common. "I cannot come
with you right now, not as beaten up as I am right
now," she says regretfully, explaining why it's Stacey
who will be leading the way.

"Team up, two in each bubble. One using the
air mark to make and hold the bubble, and the
other using the water mark to manoeuvre it
forward. If anything goes wrong, you turn back,"
Daniels orders, and I know we should be focused on
the plan, but hearing him being all bossy turns me
on and totally distracts me for far too long.

"I don't have the water or air mark," one of the

men says, and I finally force my eyes away from Daniels to deal with the next problem. The man doesn't look in good enough shape to fight anyway, with a large cut on his head, blood and bruises on his arms. I glance around the room, seeing how nearly all the people are in this state. We've healed those of them that had critical wounds, but they all still need rest and time, which is something we can't give them. My dads catch my eye, all three of them standing together and talking quietly. Dad P smiles gently at me, before going back to the conversation. How can I let my dads walk into a fight when they need rest? But I can't walk in there alone either, or my father will just kill me. I guess no part of this situation is easy on anyone.

"Then you can't come with us," Enzo says simply, and I see the man look down, disappointed I bet. I'm sure he wants to fight, to avenge whoever my father has taken from him, and instead of that, he is forced to stay here. I would hate to be side-lined like that, and guilt fills me as I think of East, unconscious upstairs. I'm sure he wanted to help me avenge Ryan, his best friend, but if the choice is me or him…it's going to be me, every damn time. East is worth more than I am.

"I will stay and wait for your word," the man

says, accepting the new plan. I pull my bag off my back, getting out my silver tube and slipping it into my pocket. I walk over to him and hold my bag out to him. He accepts it, giving me a questioning look.

"What's in this bag, my father can never get hold of or know of its existence. It's too important. If we don't make it back and we lose today, chuck that bag in the ocean, and don't look back. Never mention the bag to anyone, and you run. Promise me?" I ask, not specifying what is so important. I've left the book in the bag, which he would find easily by looking, but I don't care if he knows. All of the people left in this room are the only ones we can trust. It's not like I can take it with me; my father can't have the information it holds. It's better to leave it with someone rather than just hiding it in the house like I had initially planned.

"I promise," the man says, looking relieved that he can do something.

"You're with me Kenzie," Mr Daniels tells me, and I walk over, linking my hand with his.

"I'm better with water," I tell him, and he tightly smiles down at me, worry written all over his face. I lean up, placing my hand on his cheek. "We *can* do this. I love you." My words are only a whisper, only meant for him, and he seems more determined than ever.

"Sorry to interrupt, but I don't have the water or air mark either," Kelly says, stepping to my side as everyone begins to team up.

"You should stay," I say gently, and her bright blue eyes cloud over with anger.

"I can't stay. I *need* to see him die," she practically growls out, and Taelon comes over, stopping next to her. I watch as she casually steps away from him, like she can't stand to be near him.

"I have exceptional control over the basic marks. I can take Kelly through the tunnel with no issue. I also have the ability to breathe underwater, which means I can swim out of the bubble and just worry about Kelly if anything goes wrong," he tells us, pulling his sleeve up and showing me a mark, three circles in a line.

"No, not *you*," Kelly hisses in response as I start to thank him, and Taelon sharply turns his head to her, glaring down at her as she glares right back at him.

"You want revenge, right? It's *all* you care about, so stop being such a stubborn princess, and deal with it. You. Are. With. Me," he snaps, and I can practically see the anger seething from Kelly.

She looks ready to kill him, and we can't let her do that. At least, not right now. What they do when we don't have a crazy man to kill, and two worlds to save, is up to them. I intervene before this gets bloody, or worse, East wakes up.

"Kells, he has a point. He's the only one that can get you there. Whatever happened between you two to make you dislike each other, can't you put it behind you for a little bit?" I ask.

"Nothing happened, and fine," Kelly rushes out in a high-pitched voice, and I know that voice well. It's her lying, guilty voice. I watch as she runs away, and Taelon follows her.

"Nothing my ass," Logan comments from just behind me.

"He *wants* her ass, that's the problem," Locke taunts, and I hear them high five each other as Daniels shakes his head.

"It's time to leave, now," Daniels shouts, making the room go silent as he tugs on my hand. He leads me through the door in the kitchen, and the others follow us. The door leads to a circular staircase, which is made of wood and doesn't sound stable. The staircase is massive, so four of us can walk down in a line, and light streams down from a light in the ceiling. Every loud creak seems to echo louder than it should, and some of the steps feel like they could fall through with every step. I step closer to Daniels, holding his arm tightly just in case we fall.

"How are we going to be able to see?" I ask, noticing that its getting darker and darker as we walk down. I already know when we are in the dark, I'm going to trip and fall on my ass. It's not like we have twenty odd flashlights handy to give out.

"I don't know, Kenzie. I don't think calling the fire mark in an air bubble is the best idea," he replies, clearly having thought about this already.

"I couldn't help but overhear your conversation, and I may be able to help," A voice says behind me, and I turn to see two of the Ariziadia guards step to my side. They are both dark haired, with dark eyes and similar features. They might even be twins, or at the very least, brothers.

"How? Any help would be great," I encourage them. The one on the right holds his hand high up, and five small white lights, shaped like spheres, shoot out of his hand. The other guard does the same, and I watch as he sends a sphere to each couple. The one above us simply floats in the air.

"It's the light mark. It doesn't take too much energy," he explains.

"Thank you. They're perfect," I say, and they bow lower their heads before stopping as we hit the last step before the stairs are lost in the water.

"Stacey?" Daniels calls, and she steps forward with Enzo at her side. He must be going with her. "You should go first, since you know the way."

"Yes, good idea. Though, Linda said that it's pretty simple. We just follow the middle tunnel, and don't take any of the side tunnels. She said that she's never been down either of them, and nobody has a clue where they lead,"

"Where will we come out in the academy?" Enzo asks. We should have asked before this, but I'm glad he did now.

"A secret door behind the changing rooms by the swimming pool. We will be right underneath them," she explains.

"Good. I don't want them to see us coming when we arrive to kill them all," I say, stepping into Daniels open arms. I just want to get this over with. He calls a bubble of air around us, with the light sphere inside, and we walk into the water. The water pushes around the sphere with each step as I use my water mark to slowly propel us down into it, until we are completely submerged. Once under-water I see the long, stone tunnel.

"Let's go," I say, continuing to use my water mark to slowly push us towards the academy, and the death I know is likely coming. But if I'm dying, my father is going first.

Chapter 23

MACKENZIE

"Why did you lie about East?" Daniels asks as we float down the tunnel. I don't answer him, choosing instead to look at the many passageways, the fish swimming past us, and the broken stone on the floor. The tunnel has been the same for the last twenty minutes. "I suppose I should ask if East is alright?"

"I only knocked him out. He will be fine," I say.

"Talk to me Kenzie, please," Daniels pleads.

"He knew something, and he didn't want me to come here because of it. East was going to stop me, so I stopped him first," I say, looking up into Daniels eyes as he stares down at me.

"What did he know?" he asks.

"That I might die here," I admit, my whisper feels like it echoes around the bubble as silent fills it.

"We all might die, but you will not be alone. I would never allow that," he states firmly, rubbing circles with his thumb on my hand.

"You don't understand," I shake my head.

"No, you don't," Daniels lifts my head with his hands, moving so our faces close together as he whispers. "If you die, we die. I die. I don't believe in soul mates, or anything to do with fate, but I *know* that we are meant to be together. No matter what."

"What's your name? I know it's stupid, how we've gone this long without me knowing it, but with everything else going on…What is it?" I ask, too choked with emotion to say much more. My feeling of breathlessness only worsens as Daniels leans his lips close to my ear and whispers his first name to me.

"Really? That's it? I think I'm sticking with Daniels," I chuckle in slight shock. I expected his name to be super sexy, but it's pretty normal.

"You know why most people call me that now," he chuckles, and then kisses me roughly before pulling away way too quickly. "Sorry, I can't focus on keeping this bubble up and kiss you at the same time. It's too much."

"Okay," I grin, looking back down the tunnel and glancing back at the others. I can see Enzo and Stacey in a bubble right behind us, and Enzo is watching me with a serious expression. One second everything is fine, and the next, a giant, dark-red creature slams into Enzo and Stacey's bubble, sending them flying. Its bright red eyes immediately turn and lock onto us.

"Daniels!" I scream, and his hand grabs my wrist tightly. "What the hell is that?" I all but screech, as we try and push our bubble further away from it.

"I don't know, but with those teeth, I really don't think we should stay to find out," he replies in a hurried voice. I glance at the jaw of the sea beast and feel my heart hammer in my chest as I do. Daniels wasn't kidding.

The dark-red creature swims towards us, practically making a beeline, as we try and retreat. The others that were behind us are all rushing back towards Linda's basement too. I notice that Taelon has thrown Kelly over his damn shoulder and is pushing their bubble right over the other's heads, rushing them both out of the way of the creature. From the sight of her wriggling form, I'd be willing to bet that she's not particularly thrilled about it.

However, I'm not sure if it's the leaving everyone else behind, or the fact he's manhandling her that's pushing her buttons more.

"Stop staring, and help push the bubble, Kenzie!" Daniels snaps, pulling my attention back to the fact we're being chased by a freaking sea monster. *Funny how Linda forgot to mention that part when explaining the tunnels to Stacey.*

I'm about to glance over my shoulder behind us at the monster, when I feel it crash into our air bubble, popping it right open. As the water crashes into us, Daniels loses his grip on my wrist, and he is knocked away from me by the tail of the creature. I swim down, glad to have my marks back and not need anyone else's help to breathe down here. I swim down, trying to get out of the monster's sight, before looking back up, trying to spot the others.

I can't see everyone, but it looks as if the monster is just popping the bubbles. Nobody looks like they're missing a chuck, anyway. Spotting a ledge leading out of the water near the far end of the tunnel, I swim towards it, and hope the others will see it and head there too.

Placing my feet finally on solid ground, I walk up until I'm out of the water completely and take in deep breath. I choke, instantly regretting it, as

I'm hit by a terrible, pungent smell, one much like rotting food. Switching to just breathing shallow breaths from my mouth, I pinch my nose tightly as I look out to see if any of the others have found their way here. When I see nobody coming from the water, I turn to see if Enzo or Stacey already have made it up here. Spotting a flicker of material swishing around a corner and darting through a gap in the stone walls of this underwater cave, I decide to follow it. *What's the worst that could happen?*

I stumble through the darkness, using my newly improved transmutation mark to adjust my eyes to an animal with better night vision. I switch through a few different animals before settling on an owl's eyes, finding them the clearest in the darkness. I try not to dwell on the fact I probably look like an anime character right now.

I considered using an orb of light, having quickly realised I have the ability too. My instincts seem to just to know what my new marks can do for me. However, I decide against it, just in case whoever I'm following isn't friendly.

I follow the figure through twists and turns, never quite able to see the form I'm following fully, just swishes of material. At one point, I think I see a women's hand, but as I start running, trying to catch up, I catch a glimpse of what looks like a fin.

I see light up ahead and slow my pace, taking deep breaths as I prepare myself for whatever might be waiting around the corner. The smell is even worse here, though, which doesn't make the breaths particularly easy.

I step out of the hidden passage and into the light. My eyes instantly land on the woman, or creature rather that stands before me. With long flowing golden hair, a female-like body, but covered in scales, and with fins jutting out of her body, she's something I've never seen or heard of before. I wouldn't call her a mermaid, more of a cross between a sea monster and a human, rather than a human and a fish.

"My name is Makara, and I am the guardian of this temple. The question is, who are you?" she asks me directly, and I gape at her.

"Temple? I'm just trying to get into the school!" I reply, looking around. It doesn't really look much like a temple down here, just lots of fish bones, and a girl that's apparently half-sushi.

"You wish to go above?" she asks, and I nod my head mutely. "You cannot. You must go back the way you came. There is no way to the school above from here," she says firmly, staring at me with narrowed, black eyes.

"A woman sent me this way. She says that she used to take the passageway through here to the school," I say timidly, trying to see if the sea-woman will budge.

"Linda?" she asks in response.

"Yes, her! She said there was a passage here. She didn't mention you, though. Or the sea monster," I mutter.

"Ceirean."

"What?"

"He's not a sea monster. His name is Ceirean, and he is harmless. He does not harm those from land, and he only feeds on small fish," she says, moving closer to me.

I step back and throw up my hands in front of me. "Sorry, I didn't mean to insult your pet."

"He is not a pet. He's my helper in protecting the temple," she insists, and I look around the barren cave doubtfully again. *Temple. Sure.*

"Okay, I'm really sorry for intruding on your temple, but please can we pass through to the school?" I ask as politely as I can muster.

She seems to consider my request for a moment

before answering. "As you have been sent by Linda, you may this once pass."

"Thank you!" I say quickly before she can change her mind. "Do you have any idea where my friends have gone?" I ask.

"Still in the main passage, I believe," she answers. "I hope they have not harmed Ceirean. It would be a shame to have to sacrifice you all," she comments offhandedly, and I swallow. I hope like hell they haven't harmed him either.

Chapter 24

MACKENZIE

"This way, child," the woman says, flashing me a small smile as she jumps into the water, and the fins on her body light up. She's kind of pretty, and if she didn't scare the crap out of me with her pet and mild threats against my guys, I would tell her so. I swim after her, trying to keep the water out of my eyes as she swims fast towards a dark corner of the cave. She stops beside an entrance, which is a long tunnel half under water and I can see stairs at the end. I look back at her as she watches me, and I notice that even little strands of her hair light up. When she suddenly narrows her eyes at me, I know it's time for me to stop staring, and get the hell out of here.

"Thank you," I say, swimming through, but she

stops me, catching my arm, her grip hard enough to hurt me.

"Did you come from Ariziadia? You smell of my home," she almost hisses, leaning closer, and I swear she's sniffing me.

"No, I'm from Earth, but I've been to Ariziadia recently, when I opened a portal," I tell her, trying to pull my arm away, but it's useless as she holds on so tight that I can feel her nails digging into my skin.

"Thank you for the information, Earth child of mine," she lets go of me suddenly, watching me with calculating eyes. "You should leave now, but we will see each other again soon."

"Sure," I fake a smile at the creepy ass woman and swim through the entrance towards the stairs. I will have to ask Daniels if he knows anything about the creepy girl later. *That is, if I get a later.* When I look back over my shoulder, the entrance is gone and in its place is a cave wall. *What the hell?* I shake my head in an attempt to forget what just happened. I focus on making it to the steps at the end of this cave and what lies at the top of them. I pull myself out the water, lying back on the stone steps for a second to catch my breath before standing up and looking around. The stone steps lead up towards an old, stone door. I try not to worry about the others when I think about what I'm going to do. I *could* make a portal to them, but they might be back at the house, and we won't get another chance to kill Alaric like the one we have right now.

"I'm sorry," I whisper into the darkness. I know they can't hear me, but I feel like I need to say it anyway, even if the silence of the cave is my only answer. I swallow the fear building up in my throat and call my air mark, drying my hair and my clothes. I remove the tube from my pocket and hold it at my side, knowing it's the only weapon, other than my marks, that I have right now. My father has so many followers, and I have to fight any I encounter all on my own. If I can be sneaky and just find my father, maybe he will fight me alone. Well, that's the plan for now. I run up the steps, searching the old stone door for a handle or something, but it's smooth everywhere. Shit.

A mark on the back of my leg starts feeling warm as I press my hand on the stone. I close my eyes, calling on a mark I haven't even seen yet. When I open my eyes, there's a translucent space in the door, and I can see through to the other side. I put my hand through it and feel the cold wash of the magic holding the space open.

"Damn, that's cool. A walk-through walls mark, awesome," I whisper, pulling my hand out and peering into what looks like a store cupboard on the other side of the wall. It looks safe enough. I step through the door, closing my eyes at the feel of the cold magic spreading all over me like glue, and then suddenly it's gone. I find myself standing in the store cupboard surrounded by brooms, cleaning products on shelves, and a few cloaks hung up on the wall. I grab a cloak and clip it over me, pulling the hood up. I need to remain unrecognised as long as I can. Walking over to the small wooden door, I painstakingly twist the handle and peek my head out to see an empty corridor. I realise I'm in the hall where the head teachers' offices are located. I know this place well, I visited often enough in my first week. I watch carefully for a few moments, waiting to see if anyone comes out. When no one does, I step out and quietly shut the door behind me.

I edge past the rooms, making sure to use my air mark to ensure my footsteps are silent as I get to the hall door. There is glass near the top, so I call my air mark and float up, slowing myself down near the glass so I can see what awaits me on the other side. The sight of my mother gives me pause. She's standing in the middle of the room, arguing with my father, but I can't hear what they're saying.

There are three guards at the door, watching the argument. My mother's hands are in cuffs, which Alaric undoes as I assume he tries to reason with her. The bruises and cuts on her face suggest she hasn't been cooperating. *That's my mum.* My mother spits in his face, slapping him the moment she is freed, and he throws her into the wall with a blast of air. *That's it, he is not taking my mother from me, too.* I float back down and slam the door open with my hands. I throw a wave of water at the guards before they can even react, sending them flying through the door behind them. Closing the doors with my air mark, I throw up a barrier in front of it, so they can't get back in. *Damn, I'm so much more powerful than before.* Looking back at my father, he has a tight grip on my mother and a knife held to her throat.

"Hello, Mackenzie. I have to admit, you have surprised me," Alaric says with a cruel chuckle. I begin to walk to the middle of the room, and his laugh stops suddenly. "Not another step or I *will* kill her," he warns me, and I stop, frozen on the spot as my mother's worried eyes meet mine. I force myself to keep my focus on Alaric and not her. This is between me and him, and he knows it.

"Did you really think I would be so easy to get rid of? That you could just throw me into another world and be done with me?" I ask, tilting my head to the side. "In fact, I should probably thank you for that. Ariziadia proved to be *very* useful."

"Did it now? The water proved itself useful to me as well," he boasts.

"Then fight me. Put my mother down, man up, and fight me alone! Everyone says you are a coward, hiding behind others and having them do your dirty work. Prove that you are not," I shout at him, and he chuckles, keeping his expression neutral. He kisses my mother's cheek, as she wriggles to get free.

"When this disappointment of a child is gone, much like the first child, we can have others that will be more powerful. Do not hate me for this my love," he whispers lovingly, and it makes me feel sick. He is really that twisted he doesn't realise just how much she despises him, or maybe he knows but just doesn't care.

"Go and fuck yourself. I will kill you for Ryan! I will kill you for every vile thing you've done, you evil bastard!" My mother screams, and Alaric whacks her on the back of the head with the knife, letting her body fall to the floor with a loud thud.

"Does all of this truly mean more to you than anything? Did killing Ryan, your own son, not even bother you?" I ask, wanting to see if he has any remorse for what he did.

"No. My mission–"

"Will have been pointless when I kill you. You will be remembered as the crazy fool who tried to take over and failed. You will have nothing, and you will *be* nothing!" I say, pushing my intent into the tube, and the spear shoots out.

"Nothing is pointless when it comes to making a better world. Ryan will always be remembered as the brave man who sacrificed his life to open the portal," he says, stepping over my mother, and sliding another knife out of his cloak. He watches me intently for any sign of movement.

"He didn't die for you, the portal, or even for me. He died for love, something you clearly never understood. That's the thing though, Ryan will be remembered by those who love him, and will live on in that manner. You will be remembered and missed by *no one*, because no one loves you," I tell him, making his eyes blaze with anger. *Perfect, I'm finally getting to him.*

"Enough talking. I'm sick of listening to you prattle on. It's time to end this, and I will never have to hear about my pathetic excuse of daughter, Mackenzie Crowe, ever again!" he growls out, and I laugh.

"Bring it on, old man," I say, waving a hand and knowing that one way or another, Alaric will die tonight. Even if it kills me in the process.

Chapter 25

MACKENZIE

*W*asting no more time talking about it, I launch myself at him with the spear in my hand. I lift the spear, and send it flying straight into his chest. He looks down at the spear embedded there and laughs, as his form flickers in front of me. It's then I realise the laughter isn't coming from in front of me, but behind.

I whirl around to face him, seeing him leaning against the wall casually. My eyes dart around again, seeing the flickering form vanish completely.

"How?" I question in disbelief as I face him again, the word slipping out even though I wish it didn't.

"Foolish girl. You didn't think you were the only one to gain more powers, did you? The water in the pool here is now supercharged with magic from Ariziadia, and I have powers most don't even know exist," he explains condescendingly, a smug smirk on his face. He lifts his hand and sends me flying back before I have chance to counter it. I manage to soften the blow of my fall with my air mark, but once I stand back up, he's vanished, and I can't see him anywhere. For a moment, I think he may have fled, but then I hear soft footsteps crossing the room towards me. I stand still, darting my eyes around for show while I try to listen carefully. I don't want to give away that I know his game.

I'd wanted to just get this over with, to quickly strike him down and finish this once and for all. However, he seems content to drag this out, toying with me like a cat does with a mouse. What he doesn't seem to realise is that I'm not a helpless little mouse to be played with at all. I'm his death.

Calling on my mind reading mark, I delve into his mind and see the attack in his mind just moments before he acts on it. I spin out of the way of his invisible blow, calling on my fire mark as I lift my free hand up in his direction. I shoot a streak of fire right at him, and watch as the flames catch onto his invisible frame. They light him up for a second, before he douses them with his own powers, removing him from my visibility once more.

I grip my spear tighter as I feel a bead of sweat roll down the back of my neck. With the sound of my blood pumping filling my ears from all the adrenaline, I don't hear him as he creeps back up on me from behind. He forgoes using his powers and strikes me with a fist to the back of my head. I yelp, stumbling forward as my free hand immediately goes to the back of my head, clutching where the pain is radiating from. Not giving me a moment to recuperate, I feel an ice cold chill wash over me, as he freezes me over with ice. Stuck and completely frozen by his attack, I glare at him when he becomes visible again, striding towards me confidently, but I'm not down yet.

Using my fire mark, I quickly heat up the ice and melt it in fractions of a second, releasing myself. I dive quickly to the left to dodge him throwing a wooden chair at me, using his air mark to move it.

Sick of being on the defensive, I try and make my attack. I pull on my earth mark, using it to crack the stone floor beneath us. The ceiling above us begins to crumble, sending down rubble all around us. I use my power to keep all the debris off myself and my mum, who is still lying unconscious on the other side of the room.

The whole damn building shakes with my power, and Alaric stumbles a little but somehow remains upright. His face looks twisted as he lifts his hands up in my direction. Before he can strike again, I quickly call on one of my new marks, allowing my instincts to guide me.

The sound of thunder rolls through the skies, and a crash of lightning strikes down, bouncing off my outstretched fingers, and heading towards him. The lightning hits him at full force, sending Alaric flying. He crashes to the floor, withering in pain from my blow.

I walk over to him slowly, victory seeming so easily within my grasp. I don't know why I was so worried; the Honzel was just testing my worthiness. What it showed me wasn't real, it never was. It couldn't be.

I stand over my biological father where he lies on the ground, and press my spear down over his chest. I look at his face, his eyes, and the dark hair that looks so much like my own, and I feel nothing for this man but hate. I push down, letting the spear sink deep into his heart.

The sound of laughter rings in my ears again,

and I feel my heart drop to my stomach. Pulling the spear from the imitation's chest, I quickly turn on my heel. I twist just in time to have a hand smack me across my face so hard it knocks me to the ground. He kicks his foot into my stomach, winding me easily as I curl instinctively from the pain.

"So foolish. Such a dumb, difficult runt," he mutters. "I'd wish you weren't mine, but I suppose you did serve the only purpose I needed from you, Mackenzie. Now that you've done that, however, I don't need you anymore," he tells me. I feel my spear ripped from my hands and thrust into my own chest. I scream so hard it burns my throat, and the sound becomes a strangled husk. I vaguely notice him pulling the spear back out and throwing it to the ground. It rolls across, clanging across the hard floor.

With my eyes starting to blur, disorientation settles in, and a chill separates me from the pain. I see a figure step up behind Alaric. The person picks up the dropped spear from the ground, and runs it right through him from behind. He falls to his knees, looking up at the woman standing tall behind him. She watches as he falls to the ground, but then instantly turns to me, leaving him to struggle and die alone.

She rushes to my side, and I can see her putting her hands on me, but I can't feel the sensation of it. Numbness has overtaken my body. Unintelligible words and screams meet my ears, but I can't make sense of any of them as everything seems to fade in and out. I desperately try to hold on to everything around me. I try to hold on to the smell of my mother's favourite perfume, and sounds I can't quite make out what they are, but I cling to them anyway. I won't just give up. I can't.

I feel others stepping closer, and warmth surrounds me as I hear more noise coming from them all.

I see a flicker of blonde hair hovering over me, and I look past Kelly's shoulder, to see Ryan standing there with a sorrowful expression on his face. I try to stand and go to him, but he shakes his head. I his lips moving, and just about make out what he's mouthing to me, 'Not yet.'

Bright white light erupts over me, flowing from Kelly's hands. I'm filled with warmth, and then the pain comes back, making me cry out in agony. I feel hands grab mine, as another hand strokes my hair gently.

"Hold on, Crowe. Don't you dare leave us yet,"

I hear a voice whisper from by my head. *Enzo. He's here.*

Through the misery, I turn my head to look down, seeing the twins on one side of me, and East and Daniels on the other. Logan holds one of my hands, and East the other. Their worried expressions all imitate each other.

"Work faster. Don't you dare let us fucking lose her," a pained voice growls at Kelly.

"Don't you shout at her, Daniels. She needs to concentrate," East's voice snaps back at him. I notice that I'm hearing more clearly, and my vision is much more in focus.

"Stop... fighting..." I just about mumble. I hear my mum's gasp of breath. She's suddenly shoving the guys out of the way and crushing me to her chest in a hug. I choke a little. "Ease up a little, I almost died you know," I grumble, feeling dizzy from being pulled up into a sitting position so quickly. She kisses my head and gives me one last squeeze.

"That's why I'm holding so tight, sweetie," she says through tears. I watch as she lets go of me and grabs Kelly, holding her tight. "Thank you, thank you so much," she sobs, her body racking with the emotion.

I'm pulled into Enzo's arms next, as he crushes his lips to mine, before pulling away to look at me, his dark eyes meeting mine. "Don't you ever scare me like that again, Crowe."

I nod mutely. I definitely don't intend to nearly die again, that's for sure. That shit hurts. He didn't need to argue that point with me.

I'm dragged into a twin hug sandwich next, with neither of them seeming willing to let the other one go first. Logan kisses my head, while Locke kisses my cheek. Locke and Logan are yanked off me by an exhausted looked Mr Daniels, and I'm quickly enveloped by his arms as he clutches me close to his chest.

"You had me so fucking worried," he mutters into my hair, and I slide my arms around his waist.

"You won't have to worry again. It's finally over," I whisper back. He draws back to look down at me. Holding my face tenderly, he kisses me as his thumbs caress my cheeks. He reluctantly releases me, and I turn up my head to face East. I'm sure he will be furious at me, but instead, he just looks relieved. I struggle trying to stand. I'm so dizzy I almost pass out, but I hold on, feeling one of the guys support me up from behind as I stumble towards East. He opens his arms for me, and I fall into them.

"I thought you'd be angry with me," I mumble, shame evident in my tone.

"Oh, I'm furious," he says back in a gentle voice that says differently.

"You don't sound it." I run my hands up his chest and around his neck as I look up into his eyes.

"I'm furious. I am more mad than I've ever been with someone in my entire life. But I'm also so damn relieved. I'm more grateful, and I'm even more fucking in love with you than I've ever been," he replies sincerely, and I kiss him before he can kiss me, my lips crashing against his. I am sorry for leaving him behind, but I know it was the right thing to do.

"How did you get here?" I ask, as I pull back from him.

"Linda found me chained up. She used her healing powers to help me regain consciousness and let me out. I caught up with the others, and then we came to find you. Everyone else who came with us are still finishing off the rest of Alaric's followers, but a lot of them fled when you showed up," he explains, brushing some strands of my tangled hair away from my face. I look up and notice Taelon standing over by the edge of the room, leaning against the wall.

"What's he doing here?" I ask quietly, and East gives me a bemused smile.

"He wouldn't let Kelly out of his sight. He's sticking to her like glue. If Kelly wasn't still so clearly broken up about Ryan, I'd think something was going on." He gives a furtive glance between the two of them, and playfully smack his chest.

"Don't be so damn obvious," I mutter, rolling my eyes. I wonder what we're going to do now. The academy seems to be in ruins, and so many people have died or been badly injured. Our entire race is scared and in chaos, thanks to Alaric. I look up at East again for reassurance, but he just leans down to kiss me once more. I close my eyes and melt into him.

Nothing else matters right now, other than the fact that we're all okay, and it's finally over. I have my mum, my dads, Kelly, and my guys all still by my side. I know that together we can work anything out, whatever life decides to throw at us next.

Epilogue
MACKENZIE

Nine Months Later

*W*ith everyone I love seated around one large table, I somehow feel both elated and empty. We all know that something is wrong here, that someone important is missing from this almost perfect scene. It's his birthday we're here to celebrate after all, but he's not here to see it.

My eyes run over my mum and dads, and then at Kelly sitting at the end of the table. Her eyes are constantly wandering over to the door. It's as if she's still hoping he'll come through the door at any moment. I'd be lying if I tried to say I don't feel that way too. My heart feels shattered, and I don't know if I'll ever fully heal, but I know he'd want me to try. He'd want for all of us to be happy. I look at my best friend again. Her especially, he'd be so hurt to see Kelly still suffering like this.

I feel someone squeeze my hand, and I turn to face East. I knowing he's feeling this loss just as much as I am, he was Ryan's best friend after all. The one I've been in love with since we were kids, I know East understands my pain of losing Ryan more than the others do, and I know that's why he tried so hard to protect me. He leans over, pressing a gentle kiss to my forehead.

"I love you, Kenzie. It *will* get better. You just have to give it time," he whispers. I can feel the teardrops rolling down my face, and I taste them when they cross over my lips, the salty tang sticking to my tongue. I know he's right, but I'm just not ready yet. It's not time for me to feel better, especially not today. The wound is still too fresh, and it burns me deeply, cutting me straight to my core.

"I love you too, East," I whisper back. I'm so relieved to have him and the other here today to support me. I don't know what I would have done if I'd lost any of them. They have kept me going through all the pain and destruction that my twelfth mark caused.

"I know you do," he says with a small smile. He runs a hand through his hair, looking every bit the picture of perfection. A warm hand rests on my shoulder, and I turn around to face him, knowing exactly which of my guys it belongs to.

"Hey, you," I say softly, looking up at Enzo.

"Take a walk with me a minute?" he asks, already stealing my hand from East and pulling me up from my seat.

"Sure," I answer, somewhat belatedly, as we leave the room with the oak door closing softly behind us. We walk through Daniels' actual house, which is located not too far on the outskirts of London. It comes in handy, considering we're all working there now. Working for the council isn't exactly my dream job, but we've had to step in and help lead our people out from the chaos.

Enzo leads me into the gardens, which my mother has been slowly decorating with dozens of flowers, trees, and garden benches. Daniels didn't exactly have a choice when my mother asked to sort out his garden, which was once just grass and a few pots. Now it looks like you could find a secret world hidden inside of it.

"I helped your mum put a pond in, want to see?" Enzo asks and I grin, nodding.

"A pond? I think she has gone a little bit over board," I laugh.

"Maybe," he agrees, with a slight chuckle. We walk down the gravel path towards the back of the garden. There we, in fact, do find a pond, with plants and stones littered around it. There is a bench right in front of it and we sit down, Enzo draping his arm around my shoulders.

"How is Stacey?" I ask, remembering that he went to see her today. Stacey has moved into a house down the street with her new boyfriend, Tony, and we have started to become good friends. The Academy won't be opening back up till next month, so she's been around a lot.

"Good. Tony asked for my permission to ask her to marry him," he says and laughs. "I felt so old as I said yes and threatened to beat his ass if he hurt my sister."

"Don't worry, you're still hot, old man," I joke, and he pulls me onto his lap and sliding his hands into my hair.

"I can show you exactly how young I am, right here if you'd like," he teases, leaning closer and sucking my bottom lip into his mouth, making me gasp.

"Mackenzie! Can you come here please?" my mother shouts, and Enzo groans, leaning back.

"How long until your family goes home again?" he teases as I climb off his lap, giggling.

"A week. I'm sure we can find a way to sneak out later and finish what we just started," I wink at him, and he shakes his head.

"Go ahead, I need to calm down," he states, pointing at his trousers. I sigh, wishing I could help him with that problem, but I know my mum will just come looking for us if I don't go to her. I kiss his cheek and run through the garden, seeing my mum standing near the back door. She smiles widely as I get to her.

"What's up?" I ask.

"The twins are about to go and get their parents from the airport for the family meal tonight. They want to say goodbye," she says with a smile. It's good to see my mum smiling. She didn't for a while, not after everything that happened.

"Okay, thanks mum," I say, hugging her closely. When I pull away, I see tears in her eyes. "Are you okay?"

"I'm just so proud of you, that's all," she rubs

my arms and steps back, wiping her eyes. "Go, go. I'm just being silly." I hug her once more before walking in the house and searching the rooms until I find the twins in the second lounge. Locke is swinging keys around in his hand, and Logan is playing on his phone, looking up as I walk in.

"Hey gorgeous," Logan says, standing up and walking over. He kisses me firmly and cops a feel of my ass in the process.

"Where's my hello?" Locke jokingly whines from my right. He wraps his arms around us both, kissing the side of my head as I laugh, and Logan tries to escape.

"Let me go, you asshole," Logan wriggles away, as I try to smother my laughter, and Locke winks at him.

"You clearly just want another hug," Locke lets go of me to chase his brother out the room, waving goodbye.

"Bye then," I shake my head and turn around, heading for the kitchen to see if anyone needs any help washing up. I walk into the room, and see East wiping a plate at the sink, a massive pile of dirty dishes next to him. His wavy brown hair with blonde tips is messy today. He looks like he has run his fingers through it a few times, but it only makes me want to run my own hands through it.

"Hey there, sexy East," I say, wrapping my arms around his waist from behind and resting my head on his back. I squeal when he quickly turns around, picking me up with his yellow washing up gloves on, and puts me on the side.

"You're all wet," I complain, giggling as he kisses me and slides his hands around my waist and under my shirt.

"I was kind of hoping it would be the other way around," he whispers against my lips, his fingers grazing my ribs just beneath my bra.

"Sorry, but the yellow gloves don't do it for me," I tease, and he tickles me, making me screech until I'm practically crying with laughter.

"Stop, stop! I cave! The gloves are sexy!" I manage to get out, and he finally stops, kissing my forehead.

"Good, because I plan on bringing them to bed tonight," he tells me.

"I doubt any of us will be doing anything tonight. All of our parents are staying over for a few days. Remember?" I remind him, and he groans.

"My mum is going to clean this entire house

and then take you out shopping," he laughs at my pulled face.

"I'm sure I can cope. Maybe," I say, and he kisses my forehead as he lets me drop from the counter.

"Now, I've got to finish this before your mum gets back in here. Unless you're going to help…" he drawls off as I start backing out of the room.

"Nope. I did it last night, and you didn't me help then," I say, grinning at his annoyed face. I turn, skipping out of the room as I hear him chuckle.

"DAMN, when did this dress get so tight?" I breathe out as I pull the black dress up over my hips and barely manage to pull the zipper up. Kelly snickers from behind me.

"Maybe one of the guys shrunk it in the wash. I swear they have no idea how to use the washing machine. They turned my favourite green top brown the other day," she tells me, and she may have a point. We take the washing in turns because there are so many of us in the house. That means the guys do a lot of the washing, and my men are not good at washing clothes. Or cleaning for that matter. Thank gods Daniels has a cleaner that comes twice a week.

"I might get them to watch some YouTube videos on washing clothes, just in case," I say, pulling my black hair over my shoulder. I look down, frowning at the glowing purple mark on my right shoulder. It hasn't done glowed like that before.

"Hey Kells, what does this mark do again? Did we ever find out? Because it's kind of glowing," I say, trying not to panic. Kelly runs over, staring at the mark.

"I don't know. I haven't studied all the marks, but Daniels would know. He was the one that wrote that new book on the marks of Ariziadia. You know, the one that is a bestseller and every wants a copy of," she says.

"Yeah, you're right. If anyone knows marks, it's Daniels. It's just weird. All of my other marks I can just instinctively feel what they do, but this one I never figured out. It's been too mad around here with all the stuff with the council, our families, and well, everything after," I taper off, seeing Kelly's pained face.

"I get it," she says. "Go and ask him He should

be setting the table with the other guys. I'm going to finish getting ready."

"Are you okay?" I ask her as she walks to the bed and sits down, staring out of the window.

"I just miss him, that's all. Ryan should be here," she says.

"He is here. Ryan will never truly leave us," I tell her, and she smiles sadly.

"Go, I'm okay. Love you, Kenz," she says, plastering a fake smile on her lips.

"Love you too, Kells," I say, trying not to worry about her. I turn around, walking out the room, and run down the stairs. I can hear everyone in the house getting ready for the massive family meal we are having tonight. Thank the gods that Daniels has a massive, old-fashioned table that can seat twenty in a dining room he never uses. I follow the sounds of banging to the dining room. Walking in, I see Logan and East laughing as they use their air marks to set the cutlery, but most of it is falling all over the place. At some point Enzo and Locke must have been doing it too, but now they are sword fighting with forks in the air, using their air marks.

Boys.

I look over in the corner and see Daniels sitting on a chair, folding napkins up into little swans. I manoeuvre past the other guys to go to him. I see them watching me from the corner of their eyes, but they carry on with whatever they are doing.

"Hey, I have a question," I ask.

"I'm not your teacher anymore, you know?" he teases, but he pulls me onto his lap at the same time.

"Oh, I know," I say, kissing him gently. I pull back, and move my hair out of the way, showing him the little egg mark that is glowing purple.

"This mark started glowing, and I don't know what it is. Do you?" I ask, but Daniels doesn't say a word as he stares at the mark for ages in seemingly stunned silence. I look up to see the twins, Enzo, and East have stopped what they are doing to come and stand next to us.

"What did you say to break him?" Locke asks, poking Daniels shoulder.

"Is that mark glowing?" East inquires, drawing all the guys' attention to the mark, as Daniels whispers one sentence that silences us all.

"It's a pregnancy mark. They glow when you're pregnant. We're having a baby, Kenzie."

THE END

Authors' Note

If you're reading this, thank you. Thank you for seeing Kenzie's story through to the end, and for supporting us on our crazy journey of co-writing by reading our books. Thank you so much for leaving amazing reviews, and for sharing about our books everywhere. (It's so amazing to see posts on fb and twitter about the series! We get so excited every time!)

The two of us enjoyed co-writing so much, that this isn't the end for us. Despite this being the last Kenzie book, we have lots more books in the pipeline together. (Including a spinoff about one of the characters from this series!)

Our next co-authored adventure however will be

Immortal Choice, which is available for pre-order now! (It releases in June!) It's about a sassy vampire called Alyssa Rae who works night shifts in a supermarket… until she gets a sexy new boss and bodies start showing up anyway! Immortal choice is a standalone RH, which we're really excited to do as there aren't many standalone RH books.

You can grab Immortal Choice here.

We've also got another series which we hope to complete this year, a shifter one! Eeek! Her Wolves will be the first book in the Fall Mountain Shifters series, and it will release sometime in August! So keep your eyes looking out for that one!

Again, from the bottom of both of our hearts, thank you. We couldn't do this without all of your support. <3

About the Authors:

Cece Rose is the proud owner of one dog, four turtles and one annoying boyfriend.

She hails from Devon in the South-West of England but dreams of sunny skies and sand between her toes. Although, whenever abroad she will moan about the heat and the sand that gets everywhere.

She has largely convinced all who know her that she is a vampire, mainly due to her nocturnal habits. In reality, it's because her creativity only ever strikes when the sky is dark, and the stars are shining. (Plus, it's actually quiet enough to concentrate on writing.)

You can find Cece on Facebook and Twitter. **And don't forget to join her Demon Den!**

G. Bailey lives in rainy (sometimes sunny) England with her husband, two children, one slightly strange cat.

When she isn't writing (which is unusual), she can be found reading one of the many books in her house or talking to her amazing readers.

Please feel free to stalk her, in her group, <u>Bailey's Pack</u>.

<u>Facebook</u>---<u>Twitter</u>---<u>Website</u>

Other Titles by Cece Rose

The Desdemona Chronicles

A Demon's Blade (Book One)

A Demon's Debt (Book Two)

An Angel's Defiance (Coming Soon)

Fated Serial

Fractured Fate (Part One)

Twisted Fate (Part Two)

Rejecting Fate (Part Three)

The Last Siren's Song

Blood Sea (Book One)

Blood Song (Coming May)

Blood Moon (Coming May)

Souls of Creatures Series

Vengeance (Book One)

Justice (Coming Soon)

The Marked Series (Complete)- with G. Bailey

Marked by Power (Book One)

Marked by Pain (Book Two)

Marked by Destruction (Book Three)

The Grey Witch Series

Black Spells & Twisted Souls (Coming July)

White Charms & Dark Secrets (Coming September)

Grey Magic & Forbidden Love (Coming November)

Other Titles by G. Bailey

The King Brothers Series-

Izzy's Beginning (Book one)

Sebastian's Chance (Book two)

Elliot's Secret (Book three)

Harley's Fall (Book Four)

Luke's Revenge (Coming soon)

Her Guardians Series (Complete)-

Winter's Guardian (Book one)

Winter's Kiss (Book two)

Winter's Promise (Book three)

Winter's War (Book Four)

Her Fate Series-

(Her Guardians Series spinoff)

Adelaide's Fate (Coming soon)

Saved by Pirates Series (Complete)-

Escape the sea (Book One)

Love the sea (Book Two)

Save the Sea (Book Three)

One Night series-

Strip for me (Book one)

Live for Me (Coming soon)

The Marked Series (Co-written with Cece Rose)-

Marked by Power (Book one)

Marked by Pain (Book two)

Marked by Destruction (Book Three)

The Forest Pack series-

Run Little Wolf- (Book One)

Run Little Bear- (Book Two)

Protected by Dragons series-

Wings of Ice- (Book One)

Wings of Fire (Book Two)

Wings of Spirit (Book Three)

Wings of Fate (Coming soon)

A Demon's Fall Series-

Runes of Truth (Book One)

Runes of Mortality (Book Two)

From the Stars Series-

True Light (Book One)

Dark Soul (Coming Soon)

Mermaid's and God's Series-

Heir (Coming Soon)

Please continue reading for a short sample of Black Spells & Twisted Souls by Cece Rose... Coming July 2018.

Every Witch for Herself

Tapping my pen absently against the edge of my desk, I stare blankly at the computer screen in front of me. The sounds of the busy, London-based office barely reach my ears as I zone out. A hand waves in front of my face, trying to demand my attention back in reality.

"Are you even listening to me? Hey! Earth to Kayla!" Lizzy chirps in her usual sing-song voice.

"Huh?" I turn and look up at her, blinking as I pull myself back into focus.

"I said, did you get that email about the meeting in the glass room? I'm on my way there now." She gives a pointed look at the desktop, which is on the locked screen from my lack of use. *Oops.*

"When did he send it?" I ask, trying not to yawn as I stretch a little in my seat.

"I got mine about twenty minutes ago," she answers absently, picking at the vibrant blue polish on her nails.

I unlock my computer and check my emails. Sure enough: *Team meeting in the glass room @ 2:30 p.m.* Received at 2:12 p.m. An organised affair as usual, then. Eighteen minutes was actually a pretty good notice time for my manager, the creep. Though, as I look around at the desks surrounding me, I'm not sure it will be enough.

"He'll be lucky if we're all able to get there. Some of the guys are on break or stuck on calls. He never plans ahead for these things," I mutter, leaning back in my seat. I'm not in any rush to be trapped in a room with my manager, awkwardly waiting for everyone else to show up. Even with Lizzy in there too with us, it's bound to be awkward.

Ever since the Christmas Party a few weeks ago, I've been avoiding the man at all costs. Not that I'd much liked his presence before then, but since I'd spurned his advances directly, he'd been hellish. Before the party, I couldn't have imagined him being any worse than he was. How naive and optimistic of me, considering how the past few weeks have been.

"I think he does it on purpose to drag out the meetings, waiting for us so he can avoid Clive." Lizzy looks pointedly over at him as he leans down over the desk of one of the other team managers. Mindy is staring straight at her screen, her resting bitch face game strong, as she listens to whatever Clive is telling her. Knowing him, whatever he's telling her is completely incorrect, and Mindy is stuck humouring Mr Know-It-All until he goes away and she can finish her work in peace. If only he was as strict on the male managers as he is the females. I roll my eyes in annoyance.

"Jay doesn't even need to try to avoid him. Clive just lets Jay, Lee, and Kyle get on with it. They're all idiots; it's utter bullshit," I mutter.

"Come on, we better get in there anyway. Jay might check our call log, see we weren't on call, and get pissy at us for being late," Lizzy says, always the voice of reason. I *really* don't want to get stuck alone with him while he tells me off like a child for not being busy working. Considering he spends the day surfing the web and going for near-constant smoke breaks, it's not like he has room to talk. *Hypocritical asshole.* Shuddering at the thought of his slimy hands going for my ass, I dart my eyes towards the glass conference room and notice two of the guys from our team heading in.

"Fine, it should be safe now." I nod in the direction of Paul and Darren walking through the glass door.

"Safety in numbers," Lizzy jokes.

"Safety with witnesses," I reply, grinning despite our misery. I pull myself out of my swivel chair and walk silently with Lizzy to the glass room. She pushes the door open, allowing me to go first. I head in, quickly darting for the chair furthest away from our manager. I give Lizzy a smug smile when she drops down into the seat next to mine.

"Is this it?" our manager, Jay, says loudly in an irritated voice. He looks around the mostly empty board table, while the skinny newbie takes a seat next to Lizzy. I think his name is Rhydian... or maybe Gideon. I squint at him, trying to think.

As Jay starts talking, I zone out and settle on skinny guy's name being Gideon. Rhydian sounds like a sexy fae, not a skinny human. At least, I think he's human. I concentrate on him, calling on my second sight. Colours swirl around the room, auras shimmering over the bodies of my co-workers. Everything is blurred, and yet, somehow clearer. Gideon's soul is plain; a murky brown. No magic spilling from him at all. Definitely human.

I look over at the rest of my co-workers in the room. Darren's soul is dark, but has shimmers that roll over him with the magical current that blows across those of us blessed with being *more*. His magic is subtle; not particularly powerful, but shifters' gifts don't usually lie in magic, more in their physical strength. Paul sits next to Darren, a human, with his dull-coloured hue surrounding him, but Paul knows what sits around the table with him. Paul was raised by a cousin of Darren's, and he'd been allowed in on the secret of supernatural existence that few humans are permitted to know.

He is trustworthy, though, for a human at least. He'd grown up grateful to shifters for saving his life and raising him as one of their own.

Lizzy's aura is golden, and her hair always seems to be blown by an invisible wind, tossed by the current that all magical beings know, but only some can see. Her soul is dazzling, almost blinding, when looking at it with my second sight. I will never understand why she chooses to work in an office when she's clearly powerful, much more so than myself. She could work using her gifts instead of being stuck in an office with a split population

Working for a company that also hires humans sucks sometimes. No magical amenities in the office. No using your gifts on site. The red tape they wrap around us all is suffocating, but we have to accommodate the unknowing humans.

Darren, Paul, and Lizzy are the few people in this office I'd actually go for a drink with, and every Thirsty-Thursday night we do exactly that. I blame the cheap three-for-one drink offer at Rosie's. How they make a profit on that is beyond me. Our Thursday nights always end with me, Lizzy, and Paul splitting a taxi fare home and dying at work the next day. However, they also always end with Darren pulling some sexy female shifter and taking her... well, wherever it is that shifters go to get it on. Maybe a bed, maybe the woods... who knows? I feel the smirk spreading across my face as I try to hold back the snigger that wants out.

"Something funny, Kayla?" Jay asks, smacking his hand onto the desk to get my attention. I jump in my seat.

"No, nothing. Sorry." I look up at him, biting my tongue on all the things I wish I could say. *'Yes, sir. Your attempt at pretending to be a real manager is hilarious.'* Or even a basic, but classic, *'Your face is funny.'* I'm not sure how well that would go over, but it's probably not worth finding out. Honestly, if anything, his face is kind of scary rather than funny-looking. Not his actual features themselves, but how he looks at people. His eyes are like creepy little beads that watch your every move.

"Have you even been listening to a word I've said?" he asks, and I bite my lip. *Fuck, I have no idea what this freaking meeting is about.*

"Of course, I have," I answer with fake confidence, knocking my foot into Lizzy's leg under the table. *Save me.* I push the thought into her mind, and instantly I feel a tingle flow over me. My mouth opens, speaking with my voice, but it's not me controlling the words. "You were just explaining about the new CRM system that is being rolled out next week. And how we need to be trained to use it sometime before then, so you'll be pulling us out in smaller groups for the two-hour sessions," my voice explains flawlessly. I feel the tingle fade and shoot a grateful smile at Lizzy. Darren gives me a knowing look, not fooled for a second, but luckily the only one I need to fool is Jay, and Jay is human. His face turns disgruntled, clearly unhappy that his chance to get me in trouble has been ruined somehow. My smile grows wider.

"Well, that's everything then," Jay says, his voice grumbly.

"Did we really need a meeting for this?" the new guy asks quietly, and everyone turns to look at him. *Poor little human. So new, and now he's already doomed to suffer for eternity, or at least for his tenure here.*

Jay looks at him like a cat that's just caught a mouse, and I know he wants to play with his kill.

"What do you mean, Gideon?" he asks. I high-five myself in my head. *I knew his name was Gideon!*

"Um, I just meant that, um, wouldn't an email have... We just have so much backlog at the moment... I don't..." He finally allows his nervous explanation to trail off. Jay stalks around the table to stand behind him. It's intimidating as shit to have your obviously pissed-off boss standing right behind you, and Jay knows it.

"Are you the team manager now, Gideon? Would you like to go sit in my seat over there? Do you want to make the decisions on which directives need to be given in person, and which over the group email? Do you want to make the decision about which new employee isn't working out? Because I make those fucking decisions," he shouts, slamming his hand down. All of us cringe in our seats, other than Darren, that is. He looks pretty relaxed as he leans back, tapping away on his phone, just ignoring the situation completely. Jay wouldn't dare tell him off for it, though. He's way too scared of the bulky shifter. The dominance Darren lets off is enough to scare most people, even dumb humans.

"I'm sorry, I didn't mean—"

"I don't give a rat's ass about what you meant, newbie. Get the fuck out of here," Jay says, cutting Gideon off. The new hire looks about ready to sink to the floor in a messy puddle of melted human. *Shit, he can't seriously be telling him to leave-leave, right? Surely he only means out of the glass room...* "What are you doing just sitting there? Go pack up your shit and leave," he adds angrily, and my eyes widen when I realise he's deadly serious. *What a prick.* He really can't stand anyone correcting his bullshit.

"Don't you think you're being a little harsh?" I ask, the words flying out my mouth before I can crush the fuckers with sense. He turns his glare on me.

"Everyone except Miss Saren, get the hell out of the glass room," he growls, and they all hastily get to their feet. The new guy is the first out the door, in a rush to escape the embarrassment of being sacked in his first week at a company I doubt he even wanted to work for in the first place. "Newbie, go sit by my desk. We'll discuss this in a minute, once I'm done with Kayla," he adds. Gideon's eyes fly to me from the doorway, and he gives me a small nod of appreciation. I gave Jay's anger a new target —me. *He may not get fired today, but I might.* I sigh, watching everyone else file out of the room. Lizzy shoots me a worried look over her shoulder as she is the last to leave.

I watch as Jay crosses the room and slowly pulls down all of the blinds, cutting off the rest of the office to give us complete privacy. Once they're all closed, I hear the deafening turn of the lock on the door and gulp anxiously. *This really can't be good.* He strides back across the room, strutting like a fucking peacock, before climbing up and sitting on the table close to me.

I push my chair back a bit to give myself some more space. I don't like how he's looking down at me, so I tug my shirt up a little, paranoid he can see too much.

Having a curvy frame sucks sometimes. Clothes that cover and look modest on mannequins almost always end up looking a little provocative on me, thanks to my chest, hips, and ass. The rest of the world never lets you forget that when you're a curvy girl, either.

"While I'm shouting at the newbie for questioning my management, you decide that *that* is the opportune moment to do the very same?" he asks, scooting a little closer. Why do men have to sit with their damn legs apart? I am way too close to his crotch right now for comfort.

"I didn't mean to question your management, it's just that he's new. Can't you cut him some slack?" I ask, trying to keep my voice even and stay calm. My grandma always said you catch more flies with honey than vinegar, and Jay reminds me so much of a fly. Small, annoying, and pesky, they always fly around when you don't want them near.

"And what about you, Saren? Should I cut you some slack too?" he asks, his voice dropping lower, and I shudder at the sound of it. *Creep.*

"Well, I don't think I deserve to be sacked for sticking up for Gideon. He's new. He'll get the memo to keep his mouth shut and fall in line like the rest of the robots that work here," I respond, cringing at the robot comment, worried I may get in trouble for that one, but he laughs.

"I'm not going to fire you, Kayla," he says, and I

let out a relieved breath. "I mean, without you and Lizzy here, what else would I beat myself off to when I get home?" he adds, and I suck that breath right back in. *He did not just say that.* I choke on the air, and he laughs, like it's all just a joke to him. Maybe it is.

"You really did not just say that," I whisper in shock. He's been crude before, but nothing so direct, so blatant. Other than at the work Christmas party anyway. Jay continues speaking, as if he didn't just hear me.

"If you really want me to give you a break, we could continue our fun from the Christmas party?" he suggests, and I instantly feel sick to stomach. I'd assumed he was too drunk to fully remember exactly what happened, other than me turning him down. I'm suddenly right back there, like it's happening all over again. I can feel his hands grabbing my ass roughly as he tries to shove his slimy tongue into my mouth. I shove him off the desk, just as I shoved him off me that night. I'd grabbed Lizzy and left straight after, not in the mood to get drunk and be merry after that invasion of space. I look down, seeing his eyes blazing with anger from where he sits on the floor.

"Screw you, asshole," I bite out, turning on my heel as I head for the door. His hand grabs my shoulder as I reach for the lock, trying to pull me back. I use my magic to unlock the door and pull it open as I shove him away with my hands. "Keep your fucking hands off me!" I snap, storming out of the room. I realise just how loudly I'd shouted as I walk through the office, and my cheeks flame. Everyone is staring at me as I walk across the busy floor. I make my way to my desk, feeling like I'm doing a damn walk of shame as I grab my leather tote bag and coat.

"I'm leaving early," I mumble to Lizzy, feeling my fingers itch, my magic wanting to slip out. I have to get out of here now, before it's too late to hide it. The trouble I'd get in with the High Coven is much worse than the trouble I'll get in for leaving work early. So much worse. Lizzy nods her head and goes to say something, but I'm already walking away, heading for the exit.

Every single pair of eyes watches me as I push the lift call button and wait for the doors to open. I feel a small sense of relief when they finally do. Stepping inside, I keep my eyes down as I push the button for the ground floor. It isn't until the doors shut, leaving me alone and unwatched, that I look up, catching my own eyes in the mirrored walls of the lift. A couple of stray tears work their way down my cheeks; they're not from sadness, but from anger. Fuck, I hate being an angry crier; nobody takes you seriously when you start crying. Swallowing thickly, I straighten my shoulders and quickly wipe away those damned tears rolling down my face. I don't want any weakness to show once those lift doors open again.

Screw that asshole. I'm done with his shit. I'm a witch, damn it, and I'll be damned if I let a puny, annoying, creep of a human treat me this way. He won't get away with this again. It's every witch for herself now.

You can grab Black Spells and Twisted Souls on amazon through this link:

Please continue reading for a
short sample of Runes of Truth
by G. Bailey...

Runes of Truth

(Out now for only 0.99 or free on Kindle Unlimited.)

"Are you sure you want to do this?" I ask, trying not to yawn with boredom as I hold my sword at my side, resting on it and staring at the Protector. He isn't the typical type that come after me, that's for sure. Usually Protectors are all posh assholes in shiny suits, but this guy looks like a fake-leather store threw up on him.

"You must die, and I will be the one that finally–" he gets interrupted in his boring, predictable speech when my phone starts ringing. I sigh in relief, not wanting to hear that speech again. I pull out my phone and see Hali's name flashing. I answer it, placing it on loudspeaker, and resting it on the dumpster near me.

"Yeah?" I answer, looking back at the protector as he runs for me, his sword raised.

"Evie, when are you home? I'm starving, and you promised me Chinese tonight. The good stuff from Chingwa, not from the crappy one you like," she says as I hit my sword against the protector's, and swipe my leg under his, knocking him over. I kick his sword away from him, wondering why they even bothered sending this man after me, he is a worthless fighter.

"Yep, I won't be long, and I'll get that damn Chinese for you. Anything else?" I ask as the protector grabs my leg, calling his fire rune and trying to burn me. I laugh, leaning down, and grabbing his hand off my leg. I jump on him, placing my sword under his neck.

"Evie . . . what are you doing right now?" Hali asks, suspiciously.

"Err . . . nothing," I reply, kneeing the protector between his legs as he tries to knock me off him. He whines, before coughing out in pain.

"I don't believe that, but I want my Chinese, so I'm going to stay quiet. Later," Hali laughs, and then the sound of beeping lets me know she put the phone down. Good, no fifteen-year-old should have to hear this.

"I could let you go, but only if you will tell me who sent you," I say, already knowing his answer before he says it. They always say the same thing.

"Never. I would never betray my people. Protectors *never* betray their blood, we always protect," he spits out.

"I'm your people, you idiot," I try to reason with him, giving him one more chance.

"You are not," he spits out.

"I'm a protector. I don't want to do this, but you won't give up, will you?" I sigh deeply before lifting my sword and shoving it through his heart before he can reply. His mouth widens in shock, and I pull my sword out, standing up.

"Death will find you, and we will never stop hunting you," he crackles out, just before his soul light leaves his body, floating up into the sky. I remember the first time I had to kill a protector, and I saw the light of his soul leave his body. It scared me, but then I saw it as what it is, beautiful. That even an evil protector, has light in his soul. That no matter how many of my own people I have to kill to survive, there might be a little bit of light left in my own soul. *At least I can hope there is.*

"If only things could be different," I say, disappointed in another one of my kind. I pull out my pen, from my pocket, and my little notebook I carry everywhere now, ripping out a page. I quickly write the same thing I do every time I have to kill one of them that come after me. I write my rune name, the very thing that they hunt me because of. The very thing that many people now fear, and yet I have no idea what it says. I leave the note on his stomach and pick my phone up before walking out of the alleyway, and down the empty street.

"Crappy Chinese, here I come," I mutter, wishing Hali didn't love that place. They don't do the bacon fried rice that I love, or anything with bacon in it. The place sucks. I keep my eyes down as I walk down the empty streets of the small Scottish town I live in. The people here don't come out after dark, too scared of the possible demons around. Little do they know that demons wouldn't be interested in a small town like this, it's why I chose to live here. The flashing lights of the Chinese come into view, and I walk across the road, pulling the door open and hearing the ringing of the little bell. The middle-aged Chinese woman looks up, rolls her eyes at me, and looks back down.

"Hello to you, too," I mutter, but the woman doesn't reply to me. I grab a Chinese menu off the side, looking through it before looking back at the woman.

"I'm ready to order," I say, getting her attention.

"Your child called and placed your order already, Miss Evie."

"She isn't my child, more like a pain in my ass. I'll just wait then," I grumble, putting the menu back in its place.

"A young girl like you shouldn't be out on the streets at night," the woman says, stopping me from walking away.

"Thank you for your concern, but I'm not afraid of demons."

"No, your kind is never afraid of what they hunt," she chuckles, as the bell rings behind her, and she walks over to get my bag of food before I can reply to her. Not many beings can sense what I am, and I'm quite surprised a human has. She hands the bag over the counter to me.

"How did you know?" I ask.

"My family have always been able to sense things. You should be careful at night, Miss Evie.

Demons are not what you should fear," and with those cryptic words she walks away, leaving me standing in the shop alone, wondering if she is mad, or possibly telling me the truth.

You can grab Runes of Truth from Amazon by clicking this link…

Printed in Great Britain
by Amazon

36268828R00139